$\mathcal{V}$OICES OF THE $\mathcal{S}$OUTH

THE
LAST DAY
THE DOGBUSHES
BLOOMED

LEE SMITH

THE
LAST DAY
THE DOGBUSHES
BLOOMED

Louisiana State University Press

Baton Rouge

Handwritten inscription: Lee Smith

For Jack Wright, All best wishes

So good to see you here!!

Lee Smith

To

ERNEST L. SMITH

LOUIS D. RUBIN, Jr. and

JAMES J. KILPATRICK

Published by Louisiana State University Press
Copyright © 1968, 1996 by Lee Smith
Originally published by Harper & Row
LSU Press edition published 1994 by arrangement with the author
Manufactured in the United States of America

ISBN 978-0-8071-1935-8 (pbk. : alk. paper)

Library of Congress Catalog Card No. 68-28226

The paper in this book meets the guidelines for permanence and
durability of the Committee on Production Guidelines for Book
Longevity of the Council on Library Resources. ⊗

THE
LAST DAY
THE DOGBUSHES
BLOOMED

THAT whole summer is as clear and as still in my head as the corsage under the glass bell in Mrs. Tate's parlor. Even now, summers and summers since, I can remember everything. I remember the day summer started.

It was breakfast time, and I was playing this game I used to play with my mouth. It's a nice game that works with Post Toasties or anything. What you do is ask both sides of your mouth a question and the one that knows it gets to chew. Like I would say, "Name a red flower," and the side that said "rose" first won. The right side was the smartest and chewed the most, but the left was the best on geography.

When I got full I said, "What is the nicest tree in

1

Australia?" Nobody knew the answer so I got to quit eating. There were still about seventeen Post Toasties left and a lot of milk. The Post Toasties went around and around in the little blue bowl, all on their own, and the milk looked pretty in the sun. It was summer sun, hard and heavy, and hot even in the morning. I was the only one up besides Elsie Mae. I sat at the table looking at those Post Toasties, and after a while everybody came down.

My sister Betty had just gotten back from Europe, where she went to school to be a lady, and she told Elsie Mae it was early for her to arise. Betty is all right but she always arises instead of gets up. Betty was very pretty, and old.

I was nine years and two months, which is nice to be in summer.

Betty thought she wanted some toast and Elsie Mae said, "All right, Miss Betty. That's just fine." Anything you told Elsie Mae to do, she thought it was fine. That's how nice she was. Elsie Mae was old and hopped around. She had the best feet I ever knew. They were the littlest feet in the whole world, so little that when she came to work for us she had on these tiny white shoes with ties, like babies wear. They looked good and I loved them for quite some time, until Daddy bought her some new ones up in Memphis, Tennessee. He couldn't find any little enough so he had to get her some

sample shoes with sparkles on them. When the sparkles
fell off he got her some more shoes like the first ones,
and Elsie Mae's feet were always shining. The Queen
thought they were better than the baby shoes but she
didn't like them much. I guess I liked Elsie Mae's feet
better than anybody, but you couldn't ever tell about
Daddy. He didn't talk a lot.

Betty talked all the time, since she had a new way to
do it in. "Elsie Mae," she said, "could I have a teeny
little bit of marmalade, please? I think I want some
after all." Every morning Betty asked for about a million other things, and Elsie Mae always said it was fine
and went sparkling off to get them on her little feet.

"Well, good morning, Susan," Betty breathed at me.

"Hi, Betty," I said. I liked Betty but I would always
just as soon look at her as talk to her. She had been gone
a long time. Betty smiled and showed all her teeth.

I watched her drink coffee for a while after that.
She held her finger out like the Queen always did, and
she was so pretty that she looked like a real princess.
Of course, I thought, because after all she's the Queen's
daughter. Betty had been gone for so long that I hadn't
known; but now that she was back I knew it was right,
that Betty had been the Princess all along. Betty even
had long yellow hair to hang out of towers, and it
made me happy to sit and look at the sunlight on her
hair and on my seventeen Post Toasties.

Daddy came in and talked to us, but none of us said anything much to the rest of us. That's one of the rules: you have to be quiet when you wait for Queens. There are a lot of rules to know about Queens and how to act, and that's one of them. While we waited I squiggled my toes up and down to make them fast and big.

Then the Queen came.

"Aren't you sweet?" she asked. "Aren't you sweet to wait for me?" I would wait any morning, I thought, because meals, like breakfast, are just about the only time you see Queens. "I would like some Post Toasties this morning," she said to Elsie Mae. "Perhaps they will make me healthy and young and gay, like Susan." She nodded at my Post Toasties, which I was liking a lot by that time.

"Is Susan gay?" asked Betty, putting her cup down clunk. "I never noticed Susan being particularly gay."

"Oh, maybe she's not," laughed the Queen. Her laugh ran up and down, dancing, like Miss Hawthorne, my old piano teacher, when she did scales. The Queen laughed like fairy music. "Perhaps Susan isn't gay." She laughed again, tinkle tinkle. "I don't know. She may even be somber. I declare I don't know where she got it. Certainly not from me!" She wore the pink robe with the roses, and she and Betty smiled at each other. Elsie Mae went away, back into the kitchen, and I watched them. Mostly I watched the Queen. She was

like that butterfly I saw one time at the Science Fair
when Miss Little took our whole class, or the red flower
in Mrs. Tate's garden that I don't know the name of,
or anything bright and quick. Her hands were the best
of all. They were very white, with red on the ends of the
fingers, and long. They were always moving, fluttering
like the birds in the trees beyond our field. They were
like those birds, only prettier. I felt very lucky. Not
everyone has a Queen, but she was a real Queen all right.
She was everything she should be.

The Queen had a Princess, and she had a Court. The
Court was the pretty people who would come sometimes to the castle, or sometimes the Queen would go
with them. I looked at them from the stairs when they
were at the castle. They glittered and glittered, they
were always laughing, and they loved the Queen. There
was even a Baron in the Court. He was big and tall and
I liked him the best. At first I had hated him, when he
started coming to the castle all the time. I thought the
Queen liked him more than us, and she did, but then I
figured out he was a Baron and so it was all right. Barons
and Princesses and Queens have other rules from the rest
of people. His hair was black and silver, his eyes were
very dark, and you could just look at him and tell how
brave he was. He galloped everywhere on a great black
horse, and his spurs were red with blood.

The castle was big, and old, with a royal park in

front and yellow roses. It was just like the ones in all the books, except it had columns instead of turrets. The Queen had her chambers, and they were exactly right. She had three chambers for herself. They were blue and white, and they always smelled like the Queen. Sometimes I went to them when she wasn't there, and everything in them was part of her. Elsie Mae was the Handmaiden. That's why Elsie Mae's shoes were so nice.

Daddy didn't live there because he wasn't the King. He was on the floor under, in his own room and another room with a desk and a little fireplace. He didn't have a crown, or a throne, or a scepter. There was no part of him that you could believe was anything but what it was. It used to worry me a lot when I was little, Daddy not being the King, but when I got to be eight and five months I stopped worrying. I knew by then. Queens are different, and if you're around one you must always go by Queen rules.

That morning, it was a Tuesday or a Thursday and now I forget which, was very nice. I could see all the little turning pieces of dust in the sunlight. That made the sun seem solid, and I knew then that summer had really started, and I thought what a good summer it would be.

"What are you going to do today?" asked the Queen.

"Just stuff," I said.

"See?" said the Queen, excited with jumping eyes. "See? What do they do, I wonder?"

"Oh, they have a good time," said Daddy. "They find plenty of things to do. There are a lot of children around here to play with. You have a good time, don't you, Susan?"

"Yes," I said.

Elsie Mae came in and took away my seventeen Post Toasties and I thought that I would go also. When I stood up I felt like I should say something but I couldn't think of anything smart enough to say.

"I'm a real good speller," I said, mostly to the Princess. "I guess you don't know since you've been over in France, Europe. This summer I'm learning a word a day. Yesterday I learned hyacinth. H-Y-A-C-I-N-T-H, hyacinth. It's a flower. Sara Dell has some in her yard."

"Good heavens," said the Queen.

"Jesus!" said the Princess.

She laughed and they all laughed. They thought it was pretty funny, I guess, and Daddy said, "That's very good, Susan."

"Thank you," I said.

"Hyacinth," said the Queen. "Hyacinth, hyacinth, hyacinth." It was like a little song the way she said it, and at the end she laughed.

I stood in the door and looked back at them. The Queen and the Princess were talking and being royal like they should be, and Daddy was smiling at me with his eyes. One minute more and then I went upstairs and put on my tennis shoes so I wouldn't get bee-stung when I went outside. You have to be careful about things like that.

I went down through the kitchen and sat on the kitchen steps. They are a fun place to sit because then you can be inside at the same time you are outside. Until you get up, that is. Then you're outside for good. Summer was hot and green, going out in front of me as far as I could think of, and I couldn't make up my mind what to do first. A bug landed on my right tennis shoe and I caught it with my hand, but it got very scared. I let it go. I decided to go sit under the dogbushes for a while and then go down to the wading house.

I stood up just when Gregory came along. Gregory was always coming along when you were standing up to go someplace. He lived on the other side of the road from me in a nice house which used to be a barn before Gregory's mother got hold of it. It was a good barn, too.

"Hi, Susan," said Gregory. "What are you doing?"

"What do you think I'm doing?" I said. "I'm standing here talking to you, stupid." Then I hated myself. Gregory always made me hate myself because I was so ugly to him. I couldn't help it. Gregory was skinny and very white, and he jerked around a lot.

"Oh," he said in this little high voice of his. "Do you want to go over to Robert's with me?"

"No," I said.

We stood there for a while, not saying anything, and Gregory was white in the sunlight.

"Where'd you get that cat?" I asked him. Gregory had a very nice cat with him.

"Mama just bought it," he said.

"What's its name?"

"Anna Karen," he said, "or something like that."

"What a dumb name," I told him. "What do you want to go and give a poor cat a name like that for?"

"I didn't do it, Mother did it," said Gregory. He got a little red in the face and wobbled his arms around. "It's named for a Russian lady Mama told me about, who got killed when a train ran over her. That's how much you know about anything." Gregory was mad. He walked off and the cat went after him. I liked that cat a whole lot more after I knew about the Russian lady and the train. I wondered why she didn't run when she saw that train coming at her.

I walked down the hill, past the white picnic table and the swings that we were too big for by then, to the dogbushes which grew all along the fence at the very back of our yard. I went on my hands and knees, way under the nicest one to the place where I always sat. I looked out between the green leaves. I could see everything but nothing could see me. I laughed some, all to myself. The air smelled growing, and sweet because the dogbushes were in bloom. They had pink flowers that only bloomed in the summertime.

The flowers didn't look like dogs or anything. The dogbushes I called dogbushes because one time when I was seven and one month I found a dog under the ones along the middle of the fence. It was half collie and half something else, and it was very sick. Sara Dell and I kept it at her house. It was our dog together. We fed it soup and aspirins and after a while it got well and pretty. That was a good dog, except one time it bit Sara Dell's grandfather in the knee and then the men came to take it away. Anyway, I still called the dogbushes dogbushes. It's like Percy Q. Pinckney Elementary School, where I go, being named after Percy Q. Pinckney. Only the flowers are pink and pretty on the dogbushes.

From where I sat, way back in them, I could see Baby Julia's house and mine too. Baby Julia would be looking for me pretty soon. Baby Julia was my cousin and she lived next door. She was nice and fat and cute but she was still a baby and she didn't know it. She said she was the biggest kid she knew, which was a story, but that's how Baby Julia was.

I could also see the Tates' house way up on the hill. No matter how many times a day I looked at it, it always made my back feel funny. The Tates' house was old and large and gray. Mr. Tate was sick and never came out of it, and I figured he was old and large and gray too. Mrs. Tate came out all the time and worked on her stupid roses. She must have had a million. That's the only thing she ever did, was work on those roses. The Tates' house was a pretty funny house and I hadn't ever been real close to it. Sara Dell and I had started up the hill a couple of times, but the house was always too gray and we went away.

I quit looking at it and put my ear down to the grass to listen. In summer you can hear all kinds of things under the ground if you know right where to put your head. A long time ago I used to think that there was a factory under there where the fairies were making good things for the world, but then I knew better when I got old. It's the earth animals, like worms, and all the squirming roots that you can hear.

The Princess came out with a bright red bathing suit on and a towel. She was going to lie in the sun near the steps, so I thought I would go down to the wading house. Nothing against the Princess.

The way to the wading house was hard. That's what was so good about it. After I got there no scouts could track me down. First I went out from under the other side of the dogbushes, the side away from my yard, and under the fence. It used to be easier before I got more fat. Then I went by a secret path through a field and through the blackberry bushes which tried to grab me as I went by. They reached out their hands at me but I got away. When I came to the stream, which was only a little stream, I walked up the middle of it through the water to the wading house. That way, if anybody chased me with dogs they would lose the trail.

The wading house was not a real house. It was a soft, light green tree, a willow, that grew by the bank of the stream. The way the branches came down, they made a little house inside them. The land and the tiny river were both inside the house, and it was the only wading house in the world, and I was the only one that knew about it. It was a very special place. There were a lot of other people that lived there and they were my good friends. There was a young lizard named Jerry, because I didn't know if it was a boy or a girl and Jerrys can go either way. Jerry had a shiny long tail that changed colors in the sunlight and he was so pretty that he reminded me of the Queen. Jerry stayed mostly in the weeds but he would come out to say hello to me every time I came. A very wise old grandfather turtle lived there too. He blinked his eyes slow at me and I could tell that he knew everything there was to know. Grandfather Turtle had three silly daughters, but I liked them because they were cute. Their shells were like the rug in the living room of Sara Dell's house, brown and green by turns. The big rock by the side of the stream was not a rock at all, it was a secret apartment house. A baby blacksnake sat on the top. He was so black and fast that it hurt you to look at him. On the second floor, the sides of the rock, lived a big family of little brown bugs. They were always busy and never had much time to play. The worms did, though. They lived on the ground floor, under the rock, and I liked them almost best of all. I never saw a family that had so much fun. All they ever did was wiggle and laugh. They were very gay.

After I said hi to everybody in the wading house I liked to sit under the big tree on the bank and think about a lot of things. There were a lot of things to think about then, and there was nothing to keep from thinking about like there is now. Or sometimes I would sit, like that day, and look at everything very hard so it would stay in my head for always. In the wading house it was cool and green, and I almost went to sleep after I had put everything into my head for good. But I didn't go to sleep because I got hungry for lunch. I got up and told them all goodbye and went back the same way I had come. There were other ways to get there and go back, but when I went to the wading house I always went that special way.

"Land sakes," said little Elsie Mae when I went in the back door. "Lord have mercy. You have gone and tracked all over my kitchen. You go right back out and take off those shoes. You ought to look before you leap like it says you know where."

"I'm sorry, Elsie Mae," I told her. I took off my shoes and put them on the steps to dry in the sun. "When can I have my lunch? I sure am hungry."

"What you want," said Elsie Mae.

"Peanut butter and jelly and chocolate milk," I said.

"That's fine," said Elsie Mae. "You go on in the other room and sit down and I'll yell at you when it's fixed. I am trying to make a cake here too and people tracking up all over my kitchen don't help a bit."

I loved Elsie Mae. She could say anything but she was always grinning about it, and her feet went right on tapping around no matter what.

I went in one of the living rooms and sat down in a blue chair. Out the window in front of me I could see Frank working in the gardens in front of the castle. He was always there like the flowers were there, every summer. I couldn't remember when he wasn't there, but we never said a word to each other.

Frank was a funny man. After I got tired of looking at Frank I picked up this *Children's Activities* that was lying out on the table. The Queen had put it out there two months before because they had a letter in it that I wrote. Three months before that I had had a poem in it, and last year sometime I had had another letter. I was famous in *Children's Activities*.

I went in when Elsie Mae yelled, and I sat down and ate my lunch at the brown table in the kitchen. That way I could watch her move around and make the cake while I ate. Elsie Mae really knew what she was doing. She never dropped a thing all the times I watched. While I was eating the phone rang and somebody got it, and then I could hear the Queen's bird voice singing into the phone away upstairs in the top of the house.

"Here, honey," said Elsie Mae. When she put the cake into the tin pan she always gave me the bowl to lick. Cake was always eighty-five times better that way. After it went into the oven and came back out it was good, but it was harder and hot, and it wasn't the same thing at all. It wasn't any fun with a fork. This time the cake was chocolate and it was the best one I ever licked. I stood on one leg because it was so good, and tried to lick it slow to make it last.

I put both feet on the floor when the Queen came in, but I went on licking because I couldn't quit. She had on a yellow dress.

"That was Mrs. Parks," she said. "Her nephew is coming to visit for the summer. He will be here tomorrow and she wants you to play with him when he comes."

I went on licking.

"Well, will you?" asked the Queen.

"Sure," I said. "I don't care who I play with."

"That isn't very nice, Susan," said the Queen. "I'm sure Mrs. Parks' nephew will be a cute little boy and you will probably enjoy having him around this summer. You can introduce him to Robert and Gregory and Sara Dell, and I know Mrs. Parks will appreciate it." Her voice was singing still, but a little bit farther away, and I felt awful. I always said stupid things that of course made the Queen mad because they were so stupid, but I never meant to. Mostly I tried not to talk a lot.

"What's this nephew's name?" I asked.

"I think she said his name is Eugene," said the Queen, "but I'm not positive. When you go to see him tomorrow you can ask him yourself."

"Yeah," I said. I was almost through licking the bowl and I hoped his name wasn't Eugene. How can you introduce anybody to anybody if the one you are introducing has a name like Eugene?

All of a sudden the Queen started laughing. She was looking at me and laughing, and then Elsie Mae was laughing too. "Hee hee hee" is the way Elsie Mae laughed. I didn't know what was so funny until the Queen said, "Your face, Susan! I just wish you would go and look at your face in the mirror!"

"Hee, hee, hee," said Elsie Mae.

The Queen laughed again, a little song, and went out of the kitchen and away. I went in the bathroom and looked at my face in the mirror. The bottom of it was brown like Elsie Mae's and the rest was white. I looked

like Daddy's car which was two colors. "Susan Ford,"
I said, "Susan Pontiac." I was trying out new names.
"Susan Chrysler." Then I thought about Eugene's name
being Eugene and how bad that was. Maybe he would
be a good kid, though. Anybody would be better than
Gregory and his dumb Russian cat.

The wind blew in a little bit through the bathroom
window, and my hair blew around my two-color face.
I looked like Betty some, only she was a Princess and I
wasn't. The wind came in stronger and it smelled so good
I couldn't wait to get back outside. I forgot to wash
my face and everything. Outside there were a million
things to do, and Eugene was coming and I already liked
him, and mostly it was summer.

The next afternoon I went across the road and up it
to the Parks' house to see Eugene. I wanted him to like
me so I wore my camp shirt. That day was even better
than the day before it was. They were all like that then,
the summer getting better and the days walking along
higher and higher, like the way teachers line you up
to have pictures taken. The afternoon I went to see
Eugene there were a lot of clouds in the sky. They were
white and fluffy clouds. One looked like a fish and one

looked like a movie star, all curvy, and another looked like Santa Claus gone wrong. I always used to look for God behind the clouds but I only saw him up there once, when I was seven.

The Parks' house was in the middle of a bunch of trees and green stuff, a new house stuck onto the mountain right where it started to go up. There were lots of mountains all around where we lived, only they were closer on the Parks' side of the road. On our side the mountains were back behind the little river. I liked to go up in them but not too far. If you went too far the dogs would get you or the little people would make you go nuts. So I stayed close to the tree line. I didn't want to mess with those dogs.

Mrs. Parks came to the door. "Why, hello, Susan," she said. "It's so nice of you to come over to play with Eugene. He's around back, in the garden." She opened the door to let me go through the house but I said I would walk around outside and thank you. I didn't want Eugene to think I was a sissy.

So I went around the side of the house, very quiet, and I saw Eugene before he saw me. He was sitting on top of the sundial with his legs like an Indian. He wasn't doing a thing. I stopped right where I was and looked at him for a while and he never moved. He never moved at all and before Eugene I had never seen a kid be that still. He was littler than I was, smack in the middle of the sundial, and he was very still.

"I'm Susan," I said, and walked over to where he was. My knees had trouble getting over there.

Eugene just turned his head a teeny bit and looked at me. "So what?" he said in that awful voice he had. It wasn't a voice like the other kids' and when I met him I thought it was because he lived in a city, but it wasn't.

When he said that I got mad and said, "Well, I know who you are. You're Eugene."

"You can call me Rock," said Eugene.

"Ha," I said. "What do I want to call you Rock for when your name is Eugene? Besides, you don't look like a Rock. You look like a Eugene."

"Go to hell," said Eugene.

"Go to hell, yourself," I told him. "I'll call you Eugene, O.K.?"

"Yeah," said Eugene. I sat down in front of him on the rocks. They were warm on my legs and I looked at my legs for a while and then I looked at Eugene. He had the funniest face I ever saw on a kid. It was all white and you could tell that it would stay white no matter what. Even if you tied old Eugene up in the sun for eighteen days he would have had that same very white face when you let him go. He didn't have much of a mouth and the teeth were sort of pointy, like for biting meat. The nose was little but O.K. Eugene's eyes were what got me. They were not blue or brown like most people's. They didn't have much of a color in them at all, and they were flat. Eugene's eyes looked like whoever was putting the color into them got a phone call in the middle and just quit, and then Eugene had gone away before the guy got back to finish the job. And behind that flat white were the secrets. The secrets were all there behind the eyes, and I knew that they were there without knowing what they were, but I knew that they were not nice ones. Eugene's eyes gave me goose bumps all over.

"You sure are little for a boy," I said to him. "You're the skinniest kid I ever saw."

"I've been sick," said Eugene. "And anyway I'd sooner die than be a fat girl like some people I know."

"I'm not fat," I said. "It's muscle." My legs were brown and as hard as Robert's. Eugene's legs were bones, and besides that I knew toe tricks he never even thought of.

Eugene jumped up and left me sitting there on the hot rocks by myself. I felt silly. He looked away. "Why don't you get up and show me some stuff around here?" he asked. His voice still made me jump and I jumped up, but I didn't like the way he did it. It was like he didn't care if I showed him the stuff or not, like he knew bigger better things behind his eyes anyway.

"Well, come on, stupid," said Eugene. He walked off the patio without turning around. "Show me what you do in this place." That was the thing I had thought about Eugene saying ever since the Queen told me he was coming. I thought he would say that, and then I would show him the dogbushes and the wading house and all the other places like the magic rock in Sara Dell's back yard, and we would play and be happy all summer. That is the way I thought it would be. I thought it would be nice to have Eugene stay with Mrs. Parks, because I just hadn't gotten around to showing those things to the other kids. And I had thought I would show them to Eugene, but now I wasn't so sure any more and I was sad. Nobody ought to be sad in summer and I didn't want to, so I got mad at Eugene.

"Come on, you dumb boy," I said in a very loud voice. "I'll show you our barn." I got hold of his little old arm and pulled him along fast behind me.

"Stop," said Eugene, low.

I went dead still. It was something about his voice.

"Let go," said Eugene, still low.

I let go, and then I was madder than ever. We went across the road and started down through the field to the barn.

"I bet you'll like this barn," I said. "I bet you haven't ever been any place so nice. It's too bad you don't have any nice barns in the city." But he could tell I didn't think it was too bad at all.

"There are lots of things in cities," said Eugene.

I loved the barn. It was Baby Julia's father's barn, but nobody used it except to keep stuff in, so it was almost my very own. It was cool and brown and smelly inside, and birds were always talking up near the top where you couldn't see them. It was an old barn. Even the air in it was old.

"Here," I said. We were inside and blinking our eyes because the sun had been so bright. "How do you like this?"

"It smells bad," said Eugene.

A quick little mouse ran zip in front of us and then stood still, shaking all over beside a post. He was a tiny sweet mouse, silver, and not much more than a baby. I went up to him on tiptoes. "Hi, baby mouse," I said in the voice I used for mice. "Hi, little baby silvermouse."

The hair on his nose went up and down and he smiled a small mouse smile. You could tell he would like people if he knew any, so I got down on my hands and knees. "You're a pretty little mouse," I said. Just then something went whap in the straw next to the baby mouse and my hand, and he ran away so fast that his feet were not feet at all, but small gray wings on the straw.

"Damn," said Eugene.

I jerked around. I might have cried if I had been littler, and even then I was sorry that I was too big for it. "Why did you throw that rock?" I asked. "Why?" My voice was just like a baby's and I knew it and I hated it. Because that little mouse would never like people any more. He would grow up into an old mouse, fat and mean, and he would never smile his baby smile any more at people.

Eugene walked over to Baby Julia's father's tractor.

"That's a tractor," I said, getting up. "You're such a skinny little sissy I bet you never even saw one before."

Eugene was being very still again, quiet like he was when I saw him on the patio. He didn't say anything back to me at all, like most kids will.

"Eugene," I said louder. "Is that the first tractor you ever saw?"

Eugene didn't say a word for the longest kind of time. He was looking at the tractor. "Hey," he said at last. "I bet those blades can really cut." I knew then that I couldn't ever show him the wading house, the dogbushes, or the magic rock. I couldn't even let him guess they were there. Eugene scared me. I didn't like him one bit, and the other kids didn't like him either when they saw him.

Everybody was sitting in Sara Dell's front yard when we walked up. Gregory was patting that old Russian cat on the head, and Sara Dell was swinging back and forth, easy, in the swing that came down from the giant tree. Sara Dell was my very best friend. The nicest thing about Sara Dell was her hair, which was long and light and I wished it was on my head instead of on Sara Dell's. Robert was standing barefoot, and Baby Julia was eating grass. She ate it all summer. Baby Julia never got sick, maybe because she was too little to know when she ought to.

They looked up at us when we came over the grass. "This is Eugene," I said, sticking my finger out at him. "He lives in the city and he's going to stay with Mrs. Parks all summer."

"I'm Baby Julia," yelled Baby Julia. She always yelled. "That's because I'm littlest than anybody else. See. I'm the littlest kid here. Everybody has to take care of me because I'm so little." She pulled up a new bunch of grass and ate it.

"I don't have to take care of you," said Eugene.

"Sure you do," said Baby Julia.

"What you been doing?" said Sara Dell.

"I showed Eugene the barn," I said. "He didn't like it much."

"I like it," said Robert. Robert looked like all the good guys in the movies looked when they were kids.

"Well, Eugene didn't," I said. "Eugene thinks they have better things in the city."

We looked at Eugene. Eugene didn't move a bit; he was being still, and looking back at us with those white eyes.

"Well, do they?" asked Robert. "Do they have better things in the city?"

Eugene just looked at him.

"No," Gregory said. Gregory never said much at all. "Nobody has anything better than Anna Karen. She

is going to have babies and when she has them Mama
said I could watch."

"Hey," yelled Baby Julia. "I wanna watch. I wanna
watch her have her babies. I bet I'd be a good one to
watch her with you."

"You're too little," said Gregory, patting that old
cat on the head.

"I will watch," said Eugene, flat out. He didn't even
ask if he could.

"Not unless I say," said Gregory. "And I don't say.
The only one that can watch is Robert."

"I don't care," Eugene told us. He didn't either. He
was looking away up into the big tree. "I've already
seen cats have babies. I guess I've seen everything have
babies. I saw a woman do it one time and she yelled all
the way through."

"That's nasty," said Sara Dell. She shoved off and
swung up high into the tree.

"I don't believe it," said Robert. "It's a lie." If Robert
said it was a lie then it was. He knew. Sara Dell came
back down and then whooshed back up again like
wind.

Eugene's eyes went back and forth with Sara Dell
in the swing. Her hair was out behind her going up, and
then it flopped around her face coming down. Eugene
didn't say anything at all. He didn't even bother to say
if it was a lie or not. Nobody else said anything either.
Robert lay down in the grass and picked a scab.

"I'm hungry," yelled Baby Julia. She had the loudest voice for a baby.

"It's almost suppertime," I told her. The sun was shining crooked now, making dark places behind every bush, and it was just about bedtime for birds.

"Let's play something after supper," said Sara Dell. She was swinging lower and lower, dragging her feet. Sometimes her hair was in the sun, when she went up, and when she came down again it wasn't.

"We'll play Al Capone and the robbers," said Robert. "I'm Al."

"I wanna play Little Red Robin Hood," yelled Baby Julia. "I wanna be little red Robin and feed the POOR." The "poor" was two times as loud as anything else.

"You can't," said Robert. "I must have told you a million times. When we play that you have to be a merry man."

"I wanna be a merry man," yelled Baby Julia.

"Why don't we play Nancy Drew and the mystery of the hidden staircase?" said Sara Dell. She got out of the swing.

"We don't have a hidden staircase," Robert said.

"Oh," said Sara Dell.

Robert looked at me. "What do you want to play, Susan?" he asked.

"I don't care," I said. "Anything." I was tired of the things we always played, and it was only the start of summer.

"I know," Eugene said all of a sudden in this awful voice.

"You don't know anything," said Sara Dell.

Eugene didn't even look at her. "Let's start a club," he said.

Robert quit picking his scab and sat up.

"I wanna start a club!" yelled Baby Julia.

"Yeah," said Gregory.

Everybody wanted to start a club but nobody wanted to act like they did because Eugene had thought it up.

"We'll meet right here after supper," said Eugene in his low voice, "and I'll start the club." He was leaning at us and he looked funny, like a tight rope.

"I can't come," said Sara Dell. "I have to go down the river and eat fish with Mama and Daddy and go to Grandmother's."

"You were the one who wanted to play in the first place," said Eugene.

"I know," said Sara Dell. "I forgot." She waited a minute and then she said, "I'm sorry." Everybody looked at her and she turned red. I couldn't figure out what was wrong with Sara Dell because she never said she was sorry.

"I can't come either," Robert said in a big voice. "We'll do it tomorrow night. Right here after supper tomorrow night." He walked out of the yard without looking back, kicking a rock along in front of him with his tough brown feet. Gregory went behind him holding that fat cat in his arms.

Baby Julia's mother stuck her head out the back door and said it was suppertime.

"Oh boy," yelled Baby Julia. "I love supper." Baby Julia loved everything because she was a baby. She made a beeline for her back door and the rest of us went home. I knew it was late so I didn't even have time to look at the magic rock. There was a secret force inside it and if you touched it you couldn't get away unless you knew the right words to say.

It was even later than I thought, because I ran into Frank on the way home, and he never left the castle before suppertime.

"Hi, Frank," I said. Frank bobbed his head up and down but he didn't say anything. I didn't think he would. In all the years I knew him, Frank had only talked one time. That was the day he came to work for us.

I was having a beauty contest with my paper dolls, and Elsie Mae was stringing beans. I was only six then and I didn't know much about beauty. I always let the blondes win when I was six. I think we were in the last round when the bell rang that means somebody is at the front door.

I got there first with Elsie Mae right behind me. We stood there opening our eyes a lot because the sun was in them, and Elsie Mae wore her blue sparklies, and Frank was on the other side of that door. "What you want?" said Elsie Mae. Frank never said a word. He was the funniest-looking man I had ever seen. There wasn't any way you could have told how old he was if you tried. He wasn't big and he wasn't little, but he looked like he might have been bigger at one time a long time ago. His face was gray, and his hands, and his clothes. I guess they had been on him for so long that the gray had sneaked out into them too, like breath. His face was like the man in the moon's on a hot night, the eyes in the back of the head and dark.

"What you want?" said Elsie Mae again. "You say."

He spit one time into the pansy bed, and kept his mouth in a line.

The screen door was very thin and I was only six. "I'm going to go get Mama," I said. "I reckon she'll know what he wants."

When I came back with the Queen they were still there like I left them, on both sides of the screen door, and you could tell that nobody had said a thing. Elsie Mae stood on her side of the door with her shoes shining in the sunlight and he stood on the other side, gray even in that sunlight. The Queen was lovely and very queenlike. She stopped for a minute on the second step from the bottom, and then she walked up to the door stepping like she always did.

"Well, what do you want?" she said. "My daughter said you wanted something." It was an audience with the Queen and so Frank was very lucky, but he didn't know that.

He turned his head around a little bit without moving the rest of him, and looked at the yard. The Queen looked too.

"You want to mow the yard," she said. It wasn't a question, she said it out straight. They both looked at the yard for a while and then she said, "Oh, I suppose it needs it. What's your name?"

"Frank," he said. I didn't know how he said it because his mouth never moved at all.

"Well, Frank," said the Queen, "what's your last name?"

"Frank," he said, and spit.

"Oh, really," the Queen said. She laughed her very special laugh, the one that meant you had better watch out. "Your name is not Frank Frank."

"Hee, hee, hee," laughed Elsie Mae.

"Well, go on," the Queen said at last. "Just go on then. The lawn mower is in the shed at the back of the house. Just go on and get it." The Queen was really mad.

I was watching Frank all the time. He stood there for a minute and then he grinned, with one good tooth and lots of gray ones, and a mouth that had no ending. He went around the side of the house, and the Queen shut the door and felt her hair with her hand. Frank had fixed her good. That was the first time Frank talked, and I was only six but I remembered.

Good old Frank. It was cool and green, walking through the castle yard, and I was hungry and glad about the club.

When I went in it was bad because they were sitting around the table and Elsie Mae was twinkling in already with dishes and things. I went to the bathroom and washed my hands first.

"Well, look who has decided to grace us with her presence tonight! Pray take a seat," said the Queen.

The Princess had gotten brown in the sun and looked more like a princess than ever, the princess of a faraway hot land where she lived in a round white castle and had little black girls to fan her with diamond fans all day long. That's the kind of princess she looked like.

"Aren't you going to tell your mother you're sorry for being late?" asked Daddy.

"Sure," I said. "I'm sorry for being late."

"Oh, that's perfectly all right." The Queen smiled with shining teeth. "Just as long as you appear. But tell me, Susan," she said, "where were you all day? I wanted to take you to town with me this afternoon and get you a decent haircut." The only time I ever got to go with the Queen was for a decent haircut.

"I was just around," I said. I was moving my head right and left so I could see the Queen better. There were a lot of bushes and green stuff fixed up in the middle of the table to look pretty and I could only see her a little bit.

"Don't squirm around so much," she said. "Why don't you try to sit like a lady?"

"She's not a lady yet." Daddy winked at me.

"Max," said the Queen in a not-too-nice voice. Sometimes Daddy didn't follow the rules very well and then he would get it.

"But what do you do all day?" asked the Queen. Sometimes I wondered what they would have talked about if I hadn't been there. Sometimes I felt like a Topic Sentence in English class.

"Oh, lots of junk," I said. "There's a lot of junk around here to do." I pushed peas around on my plate so it would look like I ate some.

"Lots of *junk!*" yelled the Princess. "Lots of junk! Honestly. Susan, your vocabulary is just terrible. It is (she said a French word then and I didn't know what it was). Also, you're so mysterious all the time. There's a book written about awful little children who are mysterious all the time. It's named *The Turn of the Screw*."

"Really, Betty," said Daddy.

"Golly," I said. I was trying to be nice to the Queen and the Princess and not eat my peas all at the same time. "Who wrote it?" I said. I always tried to talk about things they liked.

"Honestly!" said the Princess. "I don't know who wrote it. I mean, who cares who wrote it? What a child," she said to the Queen and they smiled and laughed with their voices going together, like two singers in a singing show. They looked very pretty and I wished I could see the Queen better instead of all those bushes.

Elsie Mae brought me some more mashed potatoes. I liked to make them go down my neck as slow as I could, just to see how slow they would go. My neck muscles were very good in summer. Daddy had already eaten all his potatoes and now he was eating his chicken. He did everything one-at-a-time.

"Just out of curiosity," he said, "who's coming to this thing tonight?"

"Oh, everyone," said the Queen. Her white bird hands flittered out and around. "Simply everyone."

"Everyone doesn't include much," said the Princess, "in this town."

"One must accept," the Queen said. "One must accept." Then she laughed and drank some water.

"Everyone?" asked Daddy.

"Yes," said the Queen. She set the water goblet down. Daddy looked through the bushes on the table and smiled at her in a funny way, and she looked back at him and didn't smile.

The Princess was talking. "You just can't imagine," she said, "how emotionally unsettling it is to come straight from Paris to here. The servants are gone, all the guys I knew are married. It's such a bore. There's not even anybody to talk to. Tom Cleveland, for instance. If I were anywhere else, I wouldn't even look at Tom Cleveland. I wouldn't even give him the time of day. I'd probably rather die than go out with him." She rolled her eyes up and stuck out the bottom part of her mouth in a royal way.

"Then don't go," said the Queen.

"But what would I tell him?" the Princess asked.

"Silly," laughed the Queen. "Don't tell him anything. Never apologize, never explain."

The Princess started laughing, but Daddy didn't laugh. He pushed his chair back from the table a little bit and said, "Pardon me for asking a stupid question, Betty, but what's wrong with Tom Cleveland? Really, what's wrong with him? I think he's a nice boy, myself. You used to. I remember two summers ago, before you went to Europe, you were out with him constantly in that old car of his. I was a little worried about it at the time. But I like his parents a great deal, and there's nothing at all wrong with the boy that I can see. I like him."

"Oh, you would," said the Princess. "I mean, oh, I don't know. I mean I know but I could just never explain it to you, Daddy."

"Try," said Daddy.

"Well, it's nothing specific," Betty said. "I know he's a very nice boy. Maybe that's the trouble with him. Daddy, he's boring. He's so predictable. Whatever I say, I know what he'll say back. And it's always the considerate, proper thing to say. But talking to Tom Cleveland is just like tuning in to the same radio station every night. I don't know. There's just this little thing inside of him which goes glug glug glug all the time, no matter what. That's the only way I can explain it. Glug glug glug."

"Wonderful," said the Queen, clapping her hands, "and I'm sure your father understands."

"An interesting explanation," Daddy said. He looked mad. "Glug glug glug. And now, if you ladies will excuse me . . ." He left and went down the little stairs to the basement where he had a workshop or something. Daddy went down there lots but nobody else ever did.

"Max, don't stay down there very long," the Queen

said in a high voice. "Please don't go into all that. You know we have people coming tonight."

"I know we have people coming tonight." Daddy's voice came up the stairs all by itself and it was pretty loud for him not to be there. "Damnit, I realize that."

The Princess went upstairs but I stayed to watch the Queen. When she smoked, the smoke came out in pretty little blue rings that turned lighter and lighter blue until at last they went away. She was a magic Indian Queen with a buffalo pipe, telling her people about God in smoke language. "Don't stare like that," she said. Then she left and I went in the kitchen to see Elsie Mae.

"I'm going to be in a club, Elsie Mae," I told her.

"Well, that's fine," said Elsie Mae. "What kind of club is it?" She was making baby sandwiches for the Court.

"I don't know yet," I said. "We're going to start it tomorrow."

Then I made Elsie Mae tell me about where she lived, which was way up in a holler with a lot of kids and other people. She told me about a woman named Amy whose hair fell out and she wore a big red towel on her head instead. I liked that story and when it was over I went up the stairs and into the chamber of the Queen.

There, everything was light blue and sweet-smelling and royal, like it should be. Little bottles were all around, and dresses like clouds on the bed. The Queen sat in a gold chair in front of the mirror. She pushed her lips together and put red on them, and it was funny to see them together, still, instead of moving and smiling. She put shiny things on her ears and pink dust all over her face. Then she combed her hair and it fell back like it was before, brown and silver around her valentine face. She picked up the clouds on the bed and put one on. It was a light green cloud like a fairy sea in a storm, and swirly.

"Could you zip this up for me, dear?" she said.

I held my breath and ran the zipper up fast on its silver path, and snapped the snap at the top.

"Thank you, Susan," said the Queen. "You're very sweet."

But all good subjects act like they should, I thought. It's a rule. They have to be loyal and true. I am loyal, the Queen is royal. Loyal, loyal, royal, royal, royal. It was a poem and a football cheer like they have at the high school, all rolled into one. Lean to the left, lean to the right, stand up, sit down, fight, fight, fight. I felt proud and happy.

"Don't you have to go to bed or something?" the Queen asked me. Then she played with her face a little more and left, a bubbly green sea queen; and when she left all the good things went out of the chamber with her and it wasn't the chamber of the Queen any more, it was just a room in the castle. Like even the beds and chairs stood up tall while she was there, and when she left they got bad posture.

But I had liked it so much, watching the Queen dress for Court, that I thought next I would go to see the Princess get ready for Tom Cleveland. Except she was almost through when I got there. I saw her put black junk on her eyelashes and then she was through and she came and sat on the other pink bed like the pink bed I was sitting on.

"You look very pretty," I said. She did too, in a blue dress and skinny-heeled shoes.

"Why, thank you, Susan," laughed the Princess. She was trying to laugh like the Queen and I hoped she would hurry up and learn how because I liked it so much.

I got real close to her and looked at her good. "You've got your hair all bent," I said. "And doesn't that stuff on your eyes make them all heavy and you can't hardly open them at all? Doesn't it hurt?"

"Of course not." The Princess smiled at me and I wanted to smile back but I wiggled my feet around instead.

"I can't even feel it," the Princess told me. "You just wait, Susan. In a couple of years you'll wear it too and you won't feel it either. You wait and see."

"Not me," I said. "I'm not going to put any of that stuff on my eyes."

"Oh, yes, you will. That's part of being grown up. You'll like it, Susan. It's fun."

"I'd give anything to be a boy," I said loud and fast.

The Princess laughed and laughed, laughing like she used to laugh and forgetting to laugh like the Queen.

"Susan, you know you wouldn't like to be a boy," she said, which was a stupid thing to say because I had just said I'd like it.

"Yes I would too," I said low and watched my feet on the floor. They looked like boy feet when they were next to the Princess' princess feet in those shaky shoes. Mine were brown and flat and looked like Robert's.

"Oh, you know you wouldn't!" the Princess said. "Just think about all the awful things boys have to do, Susan. They have to go in the army and fight, and they have to make money for their families, and they have to shave. But girls, see, girls get to spend all the money and they don't have to shave and they can look beautiful all day long and make all the men fall in love with them."

I didn't think much of any of that. I thought it would even be fun to have little tiny hairs that came out of my face every night like magic, and every day when I got up I could zip them away. Whoosh.

"But all the women aren't like that exactly," I said to the Princess. "What about awful old Mrs. Tate up on the hill? She stays bent over all the time and she has moles on her neck and the only thing she likes is her old flowers. What about her?"

"Oh," said the Princess. "Well, she's too old to count. But look at your mother. She's at least forty and you can see how attractive she is."

"Who?" I asked. Sometimes I didn't put it together when someone called the Queen "mother." I never thought that, so sometimes I would have to stop and think.

"Your MOTHER," said the Princess. "Goddamn." Then she started crying like a baby, but with big sobs that were hurting her, and I didn't know what to do. I didn't have any idea why she was crying and it scared me. Princesses aren't supposed to cry. The black stuff on her eyes got all over her face and she wiped it off with a handkerchief. "Go away," she said to me, but I hung around anyway. I wanted to say something big and wise, but the only big word I knew was hyacinth.

"Hyacinth," I said.

"What?" said the Princess.

"Hyacinth," I said again, and she was laughing just as hard as she had been crying a little while ago. Then Elsie Mae was twinkling around in the hall saying Tom Cleveland was here. I thought maybe that was why the Princess had said that bad word, but then I remembered that she had said it before he came, and I knew it wasn't. I didn't know what was going on and my head felt very funny.

I lay down on the soft pink bed of the Princess and thought about growing up and my head got funnier than ever. I thought about the first time the Queen had told me about it, about all the blood and everything. She told me that the blood would come and that I would not get scared, that I would wear something to stop the blood when it came. I thought I had to wear a bucket like you play with in the sand. When I told the Queen that she laughed and laughed and one time later I heard her telling a golden lady in the Court what I had said. That was awful, but I guess Queens have the right. Still lying on the bed, I felt myself with my hands, starting under my arms and going as far down my legs as I could go without lifting them. I was hard and flat up and down, all over. I had a lot of muscles and the stomach ones were ticklish, only you can't really tickle yourself. It's not fair. I could feel my ribs some, but not much. They had flat fat skin on top of them.

I thought for maybe the first time what it would be like to grow up, to have big blobby things flopping around all the time in front of your chest and to kiss boys, and I couldn't think of anything worse. It would have been O.K. if I had been a little silver princess, like Betty when she was nine. There was a picture of her in the den, with a dancing dress and white ballet shoes. I wanted to be like the Queen had been, if she was ever nine. But she wasn't ever nine, and I wasn't the Princess either, I was Susan with all the muscles in my legs and arms. I felt like getting up from the bed of the Princess and going to the wading house, only it was too late for me to go out by myself. So I didn't go.

Downstairs in the castle bells were ringing and the people were laughing and sounding very gay, and I was upstairs and tired. Elsie Mae turned down the bed in my room and made me go get in it. I went because then I knew that I couldn't sleep in the bed of the Princess. Only after I got in bed and the light was out, I couldn't go to sleep. I was so tired except for my head and it just wouldn't quit. I hugged John Doe and kissed him good night. John Doe always needed a lot of kisses because he was so sad. He was a little gray birthday elephant who missed Africa lots. He was always homesick and one time they put a letter about him in *Children's Activities* and then he was known in the world. John Doe went to sleep after I kissed him but I couldn't. I tried thinking about nice things like fishes and moon pies and the club we were going to start, only nothing worked. I knew what was happening but there were things I had to think of instead if I didn't want my head to blow up. It was the first time ever that I hadn't gone right to sleep and I thought maybe I was getting measles or some other kind of sick.

The people downstairs kept laughing but John Doe slept right through everything. After a lot of time I put him under the cover by himself and tucked him in up to his gray fur ears. Then I went out of my room to see what was so funny down there. I went down the hall in blue pajamas and sat on the step that was next to the top one. From there I could see fine.

The Queen was there, and Daddy, and the whole royal Court. They were having a grand ball almost, except nobody was dancing. But it was like the grand ball in the red book except for that. The Queen was even greener and cloudier than she had been in her chambers. She was a night sun, glittering and bright, and all the people were like night flowers around her. The lady night flowers were pink and blue and black and white. They were all shimmery, and their teeth were very white. Some of them looked like they had extra teeth in their mouths. The men were black and white and straight up and down. They were handsome.

I looked and looked for the Baron and then I saw him, bringing a goblet to the Queen. Queens should always drink from goblets. The Baron was the best one there besides the Queen. He was black and white like the others but he was bigger. He was taller and his hair was silver. The Baron's skin was dark, too. He always went to do good deeds and fight bad men in foreign lands where the sun was hot. He held the goblet up to the lips of the Queen and she drank from it, and then he talked in her ear and she laughed. The Baron and the Queen were very beautiful. Sometimes he would come to see the Queen at the castle in the daytime. He left his big black charger in the driveway and took off his boots with the bloody spurs before he came in the castle. And the Queen was always soft and pretty.

From the step I was on I could see how she was a Queen and the other ladies were only ladies. Their hair was big and high and never moved, but the Queen's hair was ripply and light came from it. Her hair looked very nice next to the smooth silver hair of the Baron. The other ladies were loud and walked around all the time. The Queen looked quiet and still, but she wasn't. She was always moving in small ways, a thousand ways at once, and most of all with her little bird hands.

I put my back way down on the steps and scrunched up my knees because I was getting so sleepy. My eyes went together one time but I fixed them good with my fingers so they would stay open and see. Only there was a lot of smoke or something and it was like the ball was happening inside a cloud and I was on the outside of the cloud and I couldn't see into it very well. I kept on blinking my eyes and then the cloud turned into a glass of ginger ale and the pretty people were all underwater fish people, swimming around and around through the fizz. The more I watched, the more the people went around and around the ballroom, very slow, like there was a special way to go around and all of them knew how. They had turned into a wise fish Court. Then in the middle of all the fizzy junk I thought I saw two of them really dancing, and I thought it was the Baron and the Queen, and they were very slow together like you are under water. Two really funny things came next and Daddy was there all of a sudden and then all of a sudden he wasn't.

I was fizzy and my eyes were not working right. Then the pretty people started leaving and some of them were looking up the stairs and after a while I knew they were looking at me because I looked around and I was the only one there. Some of the ladies had even more teeth than they had had before and I was trying to figure out through the ginger ale why they had so many teeth when Elsie Mae was there, and she took me by the hand and we went back to my room. She had me by the hand, hard, and we went patter-twinkle, patter-twinkle, very fast down the hall to my room where John Doe was already tucked in and asleep under his cover. My eyes still were not seeing much and when I got back into bed I found out it was because I was crying.

Elsie Mae kissed me on the top of my head and said if I would be quiet and go to sleep in a minute she would get me some vanilla wafers. Vanilla wafers were just about the best food I knew of, so I said O.K. "Can I have some milk too, please?" I asked her. Elsie Mae said that was fine and went away to get it.

When she came back, her little brown face was full of sadness. We sat on the bed and I ate six vanilla wafers and drank the milk, and Elsie Mae ate two. She kissed me again and said I was a poor baby and then she went away. I guess that was the most Elsie Mae ever kissed me at once. I didn't like to have a lot of people slobbering around on me, but I was glad then that she kissed me. Because at least they weren't wet kisses, and Elsie Mae was kind.

This time before I went to sleep I said my prayers. Most of the time I would say them, and they would go, "Now I lay me down to sleep, I pray the Lord my soul to keep," and all that. I put my hands together and closed my eyes and did everything just right. You have to. I loved God a lot that summer, not as much as when I was seven, but a lot.

When I was seven I was holy. I wanted to be a white holy lady and live in cloisters, except I never got around to it. But one day I had a tea party in my playhouse for God, and he came, and ate a moon pie and drank iced tea. The playhouse looked nice because I had cleaned it, and at four o'clock I got all the things ready. I had two moon pies, and iced tea in a small blue pitcher, and a silver tray of mints. I had taken the silver tray out of the dining room. I was seven, and stupid like you are when you are seven, and I thought that God must get very thirsty because he lives so near the sun. When I was eight I found out that he doesn't need to eat or drink. That's one good reason he's God in the first place. But when I was seven I didn't know that. All I could think about was how hot it must be up there next to the sun. God was nice. He came to the tea party and he was younger than I thought he would be. He drank the tea and ate the moon pie, and then he went away. I guess he didn't like mints too much. After that tea party I never played in my playhouse any more, because then it was a holy church. Daddy gave it away to a little boy we know, since I didn't play there any more, and when the little boy played in it it was a playhouse and not a church and it would make me sad to watch him. The playhouse had a bright red roof, but I wished God had eaten a mint. They were pink mints on a silver tray. I don't know why he wouldn't eat them.

Anyway, when I said my prayers at night I would have my pick. I always said "Now I lay me," but I could say it to the God of the Playhouse or to the God of the Mints, or to the Jesus Walking on the Waters in the picture in the church, or to the oldest God with the long gray beard on the mountain, or to the little pink baby Jesus on the table in my music teacher's house. I would pick one and pray to him, and then I would move my hands in this special way to keep ghosts out, and if it was a bad night, a storm or anything, I would pray to Jesus Walking on the Waters that I wouldn't have to get up to go to the bathroom.

If I had to get up to go to the bathroom I would

have to keep my hand on the woodwork all the way there and all the way back. It was against the rules to turn on lights. While I was going to the bathroom it was hard to keep my hand there on the woodwork, but I knew if I didn't I would be lost. There are a thousand ghosts in a house at night, and you're dumb if you're not scared of them. For one thing, there are different colors of ghosts for every day in the week, and so you have to know what you're doing all the time. I was glad when I got big so that I didn't have to go to the bathroom very much at night any more. Because there were so many rules and things and they wore me out.

I was glad that I didn't have to get up and go the night of the fish and the ginger ale. It was the night for the gray ghost, I think, or maybe for the yellow one. I forget. Anyway I was glad that I was so sleepy, like John Doe, and pretty soon I went to sleep. But I said "I lay me" to three or four of the Gods first before I did it.

I woke up and the sun was all over the room. The sun was on everything, and I could tell it was a good day. I tried to think about the night that went before it, only it was very far away with the sun sitting yellow on everything and even on me. I didn't know if it was early or late or what. By the sunshine it was late, but my stomach wasn't hungry yet, so I rolled around for a while in bed and then I thought I would go back to sleep.

Except I could hear the Queen, and she was talking on the phone.

I could hear her voice coming into my sleep for a long time before I knew what she was talking about. "Max dear, I don't care how busy you are," she said. "Please come home right now. There's no one here except me and little Elsie Mae. No, Susan's still asleep. I just don't know what to do. It's intolerable and I'm at my wit's end. It's totally beyond my control and I'm really afraid." She was quiet for a little while and then I was almost back asleep when she started again. "Come home this second, Max. After all, it's still your house. Do you hear me? This second. No, I can't do a thing with him. He keeps going around and around that little maple tree singing 'Amazing Grace' and he won't stop at all. Of course I've tried, Max. He's drunk, I tell you. I am perfectly capable of recognizing a drunk when I see one. If you won't come home immediately I'll have to call someone else." She quit talking again. "All right, ten minutes," she said, and hung up.

I got out of bed quick and went in the room where the Queen was. She had on a polka-dot dress and looked like this girl in a movie I saw one time. Except the movie girl had wet frizzy hair because she was always running around in the rain looking for something. But when she was dry she looked like the Queen.

"What little maple tree?" I asked the Queen. "Who's drunk?"

"Oh, Susan," said the Queen. First she frowned, then she smiled at me. "It's only Frank."

"Frank!" I yelled. "What's he doing? I want to see."

"You'll do no such thing," said the Queen. She blew out a match, puff, with little round red lips. "Why don't you go back to bed and sleep for a while?" It was the first time anybody had ever said that to me. Mostly they said why don't you get up.

I went back to my room but I didn't go to bed. I put on my green shorts and my tennis shoes and hopped downstairs two at a time. When I went into the kitchen Daddy was already there, and the Queen, and the Princess with a tennis racket and looking very hot, and Elsie Mae wearing red shoes with flowers on them. They were lined up like my dolls in the closet, looking out the windows. Daddy was laughing as hard as I ever heard him laugh, but the Queen was not pleased.

"I don't see what's so funny about it, Max," the Queen said. "I think it's a disgrace. Why it's practically a sacrilege!"

"You should know about sacrileges," said the Princess, very fast. She was looking up at the ceiling, which was gray, and I looked up too. When I brought my head back down she was gone and the Queen had turned away from the window and was looking where Betty had gone. "I can spell sacrilege," I said. "S-A-C-R-I-L-E-D-G-E."

"No, dear," said the Queen. "L-E-G-E." She didn't laugh, like she usually laughed when I spelled. She turned back to the window.

I went to the window where nobody was and looked out of it. There was the little maple tree and there was Frank, going around and around it with the lawn mower. You could see in the grass the long zigzaggy way he had come from the shed, rolling the lawn mower to the maple tree. He had gone around that little tree so many times that by then there wasn't much grass left at all, a greeny-brown ring around the maple tree.

" 'On the wings of a SNOW, WHITE, DOVE,' " sang Frank in a high crazy voice, " 'He brings His love, PURE LOVE.' " He took a drink from something he had in the pocket of his gray pants without ever slowing down the lawn mower. " 'It's a sign from A-BOVE,' " he yelled. " 'On the wings of a dove.' "

He went on singing and pushing the lawn mower around the tree, faster and faster and faster, singing louder and louder. " 'If you can't bear the Cross, then you can't wear the Crown. Look a-WAY, be-YOND the BLUE.' "

Our telephone rang then and the Queen picked it up. "Yes, we know," she said into it. She pulled her lips

back away from her teeth. "Max is going out right now
to stop him." She hung up and told Daddy to go on
and for God's sake quit laughing.

"That Frank, he's going to get hit by the fire of God
in the shape of lightning," said Elsie Mae. "Singing
church songs like that."

I looked up at the sky but it was a fine, morning
blue, with three or four clouds in it and no lightning
anywhere. When I looked back out the window, Daddy
was there and Frank was still running around the tree
with the lawn mower. They were both talking but the
only one you could hear was Frank.

"Yes sir, Mr. Tobey," he was saying in a big voice,
"I reckon you like having a radio star mow your grass.
I reckon you think that's mighty fine."

He went around and around the little maple tree with
Daddy right behind him. "Oh yes I am too," he yelled.
"Yes sirree, Mr. Tobey. They calls me the Baptist Boy."
He hit the tree with the lawn mower and backed off.
"Ever Sunday on the Christian Hour, ten to twelve.
Might do your soul good to listen to the Word, ever
Sunday ten to twelve."

The Queen ran a long finger down the skirt of her
polka-dot dress and then touched her hair. She sat
straight and royal with a coffee cup in her hand.

Daddy talked to Frank for a while more and then
gave him a dollar, and Frank went away. He walked

funny down the road, singing "If Jesus Came to Your
House," as hard as he could.

I kept my mouth open for quite a while and then I
closed it and sat down to eat my Wheaties. That was the
second time Frank talked.

I sat out on the back steps for a long time after supper that night and thought about Frank. I couldn't
think about him all together though, only in small pieces
at a time. All those years I had thought Frank was the
gardener in the palace of the Queen, but he was not that
at all. He was something else. And when he was in the
yard he was part of the yard and not Frank at all. Frank
was a funny thing.

I was still sitting on the steps after dinner and thinking about Frank when all of a sudden I remembered
that this was the night to start the club. I could tell I
was late because the fireflies were already out, and blinking all over the yard and way down behind the yard
where the dogbushes were. I ran all the way over to Sara
Dell's. I ran so fast that the firefly lights were like yellow
strips of air in the dark-green air I was running through.
I was all out of breath when I got there and my feet
were wet from the grass.

They were around the tree and it was like it was before, only this time Robert was in the swing and not Sara Dell. He wasn't swinging, because people don't swing in the dark. Everybody was there and I was the last one to come. They were all waiting for something and I thought it was me until I got there, but after I came I started waiting too, and I didn't know what we were waiting for.

Babies always yell what everybody else thinks, so after a little while Baby Julia yelled, "I wanna start the club! Can we start the club now, Robert? Huh? Can we start the CLUB?"

"I reckon," said Robert.

"Oh, good," yelled Baby Julia. "I LOVE CLUBS!"

"Shut up, Baby Julia," said Sara Dell and I at the same time.

"You don't know what a club is," said Robert.

"People always tell me to shut up," said Baby Julia. "People tell me that just because I'm little. I don't have to shut up if I don't want to."

"Yes you do," Robert told her, and then she put her hands together and sat down plunk on the grass.

"Sure," said Sara Dell. "You can't have a good club if everybody knows about it."

"That's right," said Gregory. "It's got to be a secret club or it doesn't count."

Everybody knew a lot about clubs all of a sudden.

But it was Eugene's idea. I looked at Eugene and then looked away quick because he scared me a little, the way he was lying. Eugene was flat on his back in the grass, and not one inch of him moved. But his eyes were open, and they were looking at the sky. Just looking at it. Only there was nothing to look at because it was a sky that you knew would rain later, and there was nothing there but the dark.

All around us the air got more heavy, until even the wind was not wind at all. It was a big thick piece of air, walking over our heads.

"O.K.," said Robert. "Let's start this thing now. What do you want to do first? Get a name for the club or get a clubhouse or get a secret sign or elect the officers?"

"Let's get a clubhouse," said Gregory. "We could use our garage except Mother goes in there all the time."

"Let's get a secret sign," I said. "I know lots of secret signs."

"I think we ought to name the club first," Sara Dell said.

"I wanna elect the OCCIFERS!" yelled Baby Julia.

"*Officers*," said Robert, in the swing.

"Yeah," said Baby Julia.

Eugene didn't say a word and in a minute Robert asked him what he thought we should do first, which was a funny thing for Robert to do.

"We shall elect the officers," said Eugene in that awful voice. He sat up. It was the first time I ever heard a kid say shall instead of will.

Robert got mad. "I don't know if we will or not," he said. "I haven't made up my mind."

"That," said Eugene, "is immaterial."

Robert didn't know what that meant and neither did Sara Dell, and even if I sort of knew what it meant I didn't know how to spell it, so all of us got mad.

"Don't you tell me how to run this club," said Robert. His hair fell in his eyes and he pushed it out and looked at Eugene. "Don't you ever try to tell me how to do things. I'm a lot bigger than you."

"I'm bigger than old Eugene, even," Sara Dell said.

Baby Julia had been very good. She had eaten three white roses while we were talking but now she was full of roses and tired of fooling around.

"I wanna be the President," she yelled. It thundered, way off behind the mountains, and after a minute everybody looked at Baby Julia and laughed. She still had one rose petal on the side of her mouth, and she was very fat and redheaded, and she was a pretty cute kid. We laughed and laughed and laughed. Even Eugene laughed.

"O.K.," Robert said. "Let's vote."

We voted and voted but nothing happened because everybody voted for themselves. Over and over and over, and it was thundering closer to us, and then Eugene really got mad.

"You are the stupidest bunch of kids I ever saw," he said. "All you ever do is vote for yourselves."

"You voted for yourself," said Gregory. "I saw you."

"That is immaterial," Eugene said.

"Why don't you learn a new word?" asked Robert, and everybody laughed.

"Maybe we shouldn't have a club," I said. I didn't want to have a club where people fought all the time. I liked for everybody to be nice to each other.

"We can always play Edgar Bergen and Charlie McCarthy," said Gregory.

"We can play King Kong," said Sara Dell. "I get to be Fay Wray."

"Shut up," said Eugene in his lowest voice. You thought you could hardly hear him, but you heard him better than anybody else you ever heard in your whole life. It was an awful voice. "We shall come back here tomorrow night," he said, "and we shall start this club right."

"Who says?" yelled Robert.

"I do," said Eugene very soft, "and you had better be here right after supper on time." He looked at me and I looked at my feet. Then Eugene walked away between the bushes, and everybody laughed and said they were glad they were not a skinny kid from the city. But we couldn't think of anything we much wanted to play, and so pretty soon Sara Dell and Robert had a fight and we all went home. Nobody said if they were coming the next night or not. I thought about it for a while, back in the dogbushes, and I didn't think then that I would go.

We were all standing on the driveway in front of the castle, because Daddy was going away. I had been in my room burping, and then Elsie Mae came in and said for me to say goodbye to my Daddy, and I went out there to do it. He had already opened the door but I ran up to him and burped really loud before he got in.

"That's pretty good, Susan," he said.

"Yeah," I said, thinking it was too. I was getting so I could make the burps last a long time and go like machine guns. "Hey, where are you going?" I asked him.

"On a trip," said Daddy, "just a little trip to do some business."

"How long?"

"Oh, not very long," Daddy said. "About a week. You be good while I'm gone, you hear?"

"Sure," I said. I didn't say anything else because I was saving air for a new burp, and because just then the Princess came running like a race and put her arms all around Daddy and kissed the top of his head. He was sitting down in the car. She was sloppy about it and I was surprised because I didn't know the Princess still knew how to run. I thought you forgot when you were sixteen. She kissed around on Daddy very hard for a little while and then she ran back into the castle, and Daddy got in the car and drove it away slow. I couldn't get over the Princess acting like that.

I let out all the air I had saved up in a very slow burp and the Queen said, "Oh, for God's sake, Susan! Stop that!" She was mad. But it was too late then to stop and when the burp was over I turned around to say I was sorry. The Queen was not looking at me. She was looking at the end of the driveway where Daddy had gone, and her little bird hands fluttered around her skirt. I thought maybe I would like to kiss her but of course I didn't.

Behind us Frank was working in the flowers. He was gray and bent over in the blue ones and he acted like the Queen was not even there. She just looked at the driveway, and then at me, and then she picked a yellow flower and went back inside the castle. I went around the castle and sat in the dogbushes for a while.

The first thing we had to do was find a clubhouse. Robert said he and Eugene had found a neat place behind Mrs. Tate's house on the hill, and we went there to look at it. It was after supper, getting dark, and Mrs.

Tate's house looked big and black and alone up on the hill. There weren't any lights turned on in it. We walked up the hill on the path with Robert in front, then Gregory, then Sara Dell and me holding hands, and Baby Julia in the very back. Eugene didn't come and that was funny, because he was the one who wanted it first. We even waited for him a little, but when he never came we left. Bushes grabbed at us as we went by, and things tipped our legs down near the earth where it was darkest. The house was old, and so gray that it looked black up there in front of the sky.

"Wonder what she does up there all the time," I said.

"Nobody knows," said Robert. "The only time I ever see her is when she's out in her flowers."

"She sure does love those flowers," said Sara Dell, "and she wears the funniest-looking clothes I ever saw. Big old long skirts."

"Maybe she's a witch," I said.

"Yow!" yelled Baby Julia, and we all stopped walking.

"Girls," said Robert in a very mad voice, and kicked a rock. That made it all right and we started walking again.

"Where are we going, anyway?" asked Sara Dell. "*The Lone Ranger's* on tonight."

"*The Lone Ranger's* on a lot," said Gregory.

"Look, you don't have to be in this club if you don't want to."

"I want to," said Sara Dell.

"I love TONTO!" yelled Baby Julia. She was the only one that didn't whisper.

"We're going out behind Mrs. Tate's garden," said Robert. "There's this little shack out there."

We went on and I had to keep grabbing Baby Julia because she kept stomping on the flowers and the Queen had told me never to walk in Mrs. Tate's flowers. Then we went under a fence and there it was.

"It's just a chicken house," said Sara Dell.

"It is not, stupid," said Robert. "It's a clubhouse."

"Oh," said Sara Dell.

"I'm sleepy," yelled Baby Julia.

"Shut up," I said.

The next thing we had to do was elect a president, only we had already tried that one time before. "I'll just go ahead and be the President," said Robert. "I don't mind."

"No, I want to be the President," said Gregory.

"You can't," Robert said, "because you wear glasses. Anyway I'm the President. You can be the Vice-President."

"I want to be the Vice-President," said Sara Dell and me at the same time.

"O.K.," Robert said. "Everybody except Baby Julia can be the Vice-President."

Baby Julia started crying. "I wanna be a Vice-President," she yelled.

"Shut up," said Robert. "You can be the nurse."

So Baby Julia quit crying, and we all sat in a circle and thought up names for the club. It was getting pretty dark by that time and hard to see. I could see Gregory's face the best because it was the whitest. He sat across from me.

"What's that?" asked Sara Dell suddenly. Something was coming up the path through the flower garden.

"Run," I said, but nobody ran because that path was the only way out. My arms and my legs were just like lemon jello.

"Who's there?" yelled Robert. He was brave.

"Me and Little Arthur," said Eugene. His voice came out of the dark beyond the clubhouse, loud, and even Robert jumped. You couldn't see Eugene but his voice was with us in our clubhouse. Eugene lit a candle, a tall twisty candle like you have on party tables, and then we could see his face. Before, when there was only his voice, I had wanted to see his face; but when I could see it, I didn't want to any more. Eugene came out of the black flowers and into the clubhouse. He looked very funny because he was smiling, and Eugene didn't smile.

"Look, Eugene," said Robert. "You can't be in our club, so get out."

"No, Robert," Eugene said, quiet, "I'm in the club. Me and Little Arthur." He sat down on the ground and smiled at us, and his eyes were big and almost white in the jumpy light of that candle.

"Wait a minute," said Sara Dell. "Who's Little Arthur?"

"He's my friend," said Eugene. "He's right here beside me." Then Eugene did a strange thing. He turned around and smiled at the air beside him. Everybody looked, and I almost smiled too because Eugene was smiling such a big smile, but nothing was there. Nothing but the warm black air of night in summer and the smell of flowers beyond, where the path started.

"I don't see Little Arthur," said Baby Julia, "and I'm the nurse."

"You're only six," said Eugene, being very sweet with Baby Julia.

"Oh," said Baby Julia, and grinned at Eugene. Then she grinned at the air beside Eugene and giggled. "Oh," she said again.

I didn't know what was going on and I felt funny in my stomach. "What are you talking about?" I asked Eugene. My voice was like a baby voice.

"Why, Little Arthur," he said in that soft way. A small wind blew through the clubhouse, but it was a sticky wind and too sweet with flowers.

"Get out of here, Eugene," yelled Robert. "Can't you see we're trying to have a meeting? Go on, leave."

"Wait a minute," said Sara Dell and Gregory at the same time.

"Tell about Little Arthur," I said. It was quiet and

still in the clubhouse and their faces looked big and then little, near and then far away in that crazy candle's light. Eugene sat smiling and looking out the clubhouse door. I looked too, where everything was night, and then I worked my big toes around. I looked back at Eugene for a long time and then I thought how bad I wanted to know Little Arthur. I couldn't wait to know him.

"Tell about Little Arthur," I said again, and nobody else said a word.

"He was there when I woke up this morning," said Eugene. Eugene's eyes were jumping out at us and we were listening to him very hard. "I woke up and he was sitting on the end of my bed and I said, 'Who are you?,' and he said, 'I'm Little Arthur.' "

"That's all he said?" Robert asked.

"Oh no," said Eugene. "We talked for a long time. I'm the only one can see him or hear him but he likes you all too."

"He does?" giggled Baby Julia. For once she didn't yell and she smiled at Little Arthur. She really loved him.

"What does he look like?" I asked. I wished I could see him too. I wished he had come to sit on my bed instead of Eugene's.

"He's real little," said Eugene, "but he's old."

"How little?" asked Robert.

"About two feet tall," said Eugene.

"How old?" I said.

"About 462 years old," Eugene said, slow, and we were quiet.

Sara Dell wanted to know what he wore. She would.

"He has on a long black coat," said Eugene, "and a red hat and big boots. Black ones."

"Gosh," said Baby Julia.

"And he has a gun," Eugene said. "A great big gun. Loaded."

Then it was like the night got colder outside the clubhouse and we all moved a little bit away from Eugene and from Little Arthur.

"Oh, you don't have to be afraid," laughed Eugene. The secrets were moving behind the flat white of his eyes. And they were awful secrets like I had thought they would be, but I wanted to know what they were, and I wanted to know Little Arthur more than ever. "You don't have to be afraid," Eugene said again. "He wants to be in the club."

"Oh goody," said Sara Dell.

"I want Little Arthur to be the President," yelled Baby Julia. "I'm the nurse."

"Wait just one little minute," said Robert. "I'm the President."

"Little Arthur would like to be the President," smiled Eugene. "Why don't you vote on it?"

"O.K.," I said. "Everybody for Little Arthur put up their hands." Everybody put up their hands except Robert.

"Little Arthur says he is very happy to be the President," said Eugene, and we all smiled at the air where Little Arthur was. "He accepts with pleasure."

"You all are nuts," Robert said. "I'm going home." Only he didn't. He sat right where he was.

"Little Arthur says that this is a secret club and that it only meets at night," Eugene told us. "We'll have a meeting tomorrow night after supper and have the initiation."

"What's a denition?" asked Baby Julia.

"Little Arthur says to wait and see," said Eugene. I couldn't wait to see.

All of a sudden we knew how late it was and Little Arthur said the meeting was adjourned. It was very scary walking back through the flowers. They smelled black and sticky and the only thing I could see was Sara Dell's shirt in front of me. I wished Little Arthur and Eugene were in front too, instead of behind us where they were. Baby Julia fell on her head but she didn't make a sound. Babies will surprise you that way sometimes. They know a lot more than you think.

I guess I woke up late the next day, because when I went down the stairs nobody was around. I ate some of the Princess' Melba toast for breakfast, just for fun, only it tasted like cardboard. So I put the rest of my piece back in the box, and read *Little Orphan Annie* in the funny papers. Little Orphan Annie is all right but nobody's hair is like that, not even Little Orphan Annie's. It can't be.

Outside the weather was raining a little bit, the gray kind that goes on all day and never stops even one time for people to go out in puddles. I thought maybe I would put on my bathing suit and go out and stand in the rain for a while, but when I got my bathing suit it didn't have any seat in it so I didn't go out. I went down to Daddy's workshop instead.

I don't know what I went down there for. The workshop was there like it always was, all the time ever since I could remember, only before this one day I had never been in it. Daddy was in it lots but I wasn't ever. Nobody else was either, besides him, but of course Daddy wasn't ever in the wading house. Or my doll town, which was the best place in the castle. It was a closet which wasn't a closet at all but a whole town full of doll people who lived in little box houses, or big ones if they had the money. I had the doll town, and the wading house, and the dogbushes, and Daddy had the workshop. Except that day when I went down there.

The walls of the steps were very close together, and at the bottom of them there was a white washing machine that was shining in the dark. It was a nice new washing machine with a wringer on the top but Elsie Mae wouldn't use it. She said she was better than it was, and left it alone in the basement. Around the washing machine was all this junk that nobody wanted any more. The junk was like the leaves and the roots and the washing machine was like a white flower above them. I liked that a lot and I couldn't figure out why I hadn't ever gone down there before.

I went over and messed around in the junk a little bit. It was all nice stuff, like a hoop and a football-player letter and the chair that used to be in the den before that skinny little man with the curly hair and the smile came and said to paint the living room another color. So they did, and then the chair was in the basement like an old man moved to Florida to retire. I thought it was sad.

There was a little road through the junk to Daddy's workshop. It was a curvy road that twisted around the chairs and the tables and the piles of junk. At the end of the little road was the door. At first it didn't want to come open because nobody except Daddy had been in there for so long that it didn't know what to think.

Inside there was only one window, high up, and the soft gray rain light from outside. There was a big table, brown, and some old brushes in a fruit jar thing on the table. There was another door like a little closet. It was very low, almost a dog door, and when I opened it was when I found everything.

The little closet was full of pictures. Some of them were big and some were little and some had wood around their sides and some didn't. Sometimes they were black and white and other times they were in bright colors. I pulled them all out, one by one, and when I had gotten them out you couldn't even see the workshop any more because there were too many. The gray rain light fell on them just enough for me to see.

I don't know how long I stayed down there. They were the prettiest things I ever saw. They were that kind of pretty that makes you want to hold your breath and cry, because it is like wand magic and you think if you blink it will go away. Before, I didn't know anything could be that pretty that wasn't alive and outside. But this was like being outside and inside all together.

In one of them a horse was on a hill like Black Beauty, and the wind was blowing through the picture and the hair on his neck blew out long behind him in the wind. A little girl sat in one picture, in a new pink dress, and in the part of the picture behind her there were a whole lot of flowers. She looked like me. Another picture was gypsy people and a fire. The fire jumped and the people were singing. One corner of that picture was raggedy, and it looked older than some others. There were dancing girls and men faces, and woods and trees, but mostly there were pictures of the Queen.

She would be different colors and turned in different ways, but you always knew that she was the Queen. No matter which way she was turned, you always knew. In one picture there was a wall, and she was looking over it, and nobody could say what she saw. She was at the piano one time, and another time it was just her face with black around; she was very fine. In all the pictures her hands moved, flying out of the pictures. One picture was only her hands. And one picture was her face a million times in a million places, over on top of each other and everything, in lots of colors. She looked so much alive in those pictures. Only she looked more than alive. She looked like she had died and gone to heaven.

I thought then about Daddy, about this being his workshop where he spent so much time. I looked at all the pictures on the floor and I thought about him, Daddy, who was good and sweet with old eyes and a little smile. He took his pills at breakfast and drove away every day from the breakfast table to work, in his two-color car. He was always the same, and he was not the King. He never said much at all. This was where he went then, when he went away to the basement. Ha ha, I thought. Now I know, I thought. But it didn't make me feel good. It made me feel like sin in the Bible. This is a hobby, I thought. Lots of men have hobbies, I knew that. But I couldn't figure why he didn't bring the pictures upstairs and hang them in the house, and then I thought that maybe the Queen didn't like them, or maybe that he never showed them to her. I didn't know which. It was very strange.

I put them back in their little dog closet one at a time. All the pictures went back in. I closed the door on them, and ran back through the basement as fast as I could go.

I fell down because I was running, and banged up my knee bad. I was happy at that because my scab would be bigger than Robert's. But I was still sitting in a funny way in all the junk on the floor, so I started crying. I sat on the floor and thought about everything for a long time.

I was glad I had seen them, all those pictures. I didn't think I would look at them any more but I was glad I had looked at them once. I had put them away tight in my head and they would stay there for me to look at when I wanted. I liked having them up there in my head.

Upstairs somebody was yelling for me. I got up and went up the stairs one at a time because blood was going down my knee in a little river, and it was starting to hurt. It didn't hurt bad though, and I felt like I would get cut a hundred times with those pictures in my head.

"Lawsy mercy," said little Elsie Mae when she saw me. "What have you gone and done to yourself, baby? You have cut your poor little old leg all to pieces."

"No I haven't," I said. "It just looks like it."

"Well it sure does look like it," said Elsie Mae. "You

could of fooled me. You sit right there, honey, and I'll be back directly with something to fix you up. Just go on and lie down why don't you on the sofa and stretch out that sweet little old leg."

She made me feel silly but I liked it and I got on the sofa and shut my eyes. When Elsie Mae came back I got three Band Aids and a Hershey bar, and Elsie Mae sat in the red chair and told me a nice long story about how her uncle got bit by a mad dog when he was eleven years old, and he went so crazy they had to strap him down. Outside I could see the mountains far away and I knew that the dogs were back there someplace but I wasn't thinking about them. Everything outside was getting washed and squishy with rain, and inside it was only Elsie Mae and me. She told me another story about a welfare lady who chased after a man she knew, and when she was through I went to sleep. I felt good because it was gray and wet beyond the windows, but I was on the sofa in the house, and under the house were all those pictures and I knew it.

Later on that afternoon it was still raining and I was upstairs in my doll closet. I was having a play and Myrna Loy was a girl spy. She was trying to find out who the Lone Ranger really was behind his mask. Only she couldn't get that mask off and she had tried everything. The play was in a very exciting part when our doorbell rang. I heard Elsie Mae go answer it. She said something was fine but she didn't sound like it, and I heard a man laughing, and then the Queen ran down the stairs. I went down too.

We all sat in the living room. It was the Queen and me and the Baron. He shook hands with me, very grown up, and said wasn't I a pretty girl but I'd never beat my mother. The Queen laughed and pulled some hair out of my eyes with her finger. She had on a dark blue dress that spread out around her every which way when she sat down. She said she thought I had a cute little face, too, when you could see it for my hair.

"I just happened to think," said the Baron, "that it's a lovely night for a drive down the river and dinner. What do you say? I feel that you should be properly entertained while Mr. Tobey is away, a pretty thing like you." He looked at me as he said the last part.

"I like to ride in the rain," said the Queen. The Baron knew exactly how to talk to her. He kept just far enough away and he made his eyebrows go exactly right, and he looked at her very close. He talked deep in his throat and very slow, so that what he said sounded like big stuff all the time even when it wasn't.

"Let me run and get my raincoat," said the Queen. "You were so smart to think of it."

The Baron stood up when she went out of the room.

He was great big. He looked like all the men in the old movies because of the hair on his face, and while she was gone he asked me how I liked school. I said, "I think it's very nice, I like it a lot. Thank you, sir," because I always tried to show respect to the Court when they talked with me. The Baron made a noise like a growl in his throat to answer.

The Queen came back with her raincoat and they left, running through the rain to the stallion that was a car. I stood at the window and watched them go. Elsie Mae stood behind me, and when I turned around to ask her something, she kissed the front of my head.

Later that day the Princess was talking to Tom Cleveland on the phone. I was trying to listen but I couldn't hear very well. "No, that's where he is now," she said, "seeing the lawyer. Oh, I don't know. It's really a mess." She waited a minute. "But you just should have been here this afternoon," she told Tom Cleveland. "I couldn't believe he would come to our house like that. It's the most fragrant thing I've ever seen." I guess I couldn't hear very well, because when I looked up fragrant in the dictionary it meant smells good, and I didn't think that was what the Princess meant at all. I didn't know what she was talking about.

That night there was a club meeting. It stopped raining just long enough for us to have it. The grass and the trees smelled great, and Sara Dell and I pulled at the limbs of all the trees so water would fall on us.

We were very wet when we got to the clubhouse. We came into it laughing but once we got there we were very quiet. We were the last ones to come. Everybody else stood in a circle because the ground was too wet to sit on. There was Robert, and Gregory, and Baby Julia was next to him because she had come up with him, and two empty places for Sara Dell and me. Little Arthur stood next to Eugene.

Eugene lit the twisty candle and we all got away a little bit from his face in its light. "Little Arthur says that we should all kneel," he said.

"I'm not going to," said Sara Dell. "I don't want tc get dirty." Her hair was long and it jumped and moved with the candle.

"Then Little Arthur says you may sit on your haunches," Eugene said.

"What's a haunch?" asked Sara Dell.

"Hey, let me sit on my haunch. Where's my haunch?" said Baby Julia. But she made less noise in the club than she ever made other times.

"Your haunch is like this," Eugene told us. He bent down onto his heels. "See? That's the way the preachers in India sit to count their beads, and then they go to sleep on nails."

"That's a big lie," said Robert.

"Little Arthur says you may be hurt if you talk that way," Eugene said, softly.

I wanted to sit on my haunches like the men of India,

only it hurt my sore knee so I sat in the mud. It was nice cool mud. On top of the clubhouse was a slow drip, drip, drip, from the wet trees. It made me want to yell or run but I just moved my toes and kept quiet.

"Little Arthur says we have to start this club," said Eugene, his white eyes looking up, "by mixing our blood." He pulled out a long shiny knife, not a kitchen knife but a kill knife, and Sara Dell pulled all her breath in at once.

"You're not going to cut on me with that thing," she said.

"Oh, but Little Arthur wants your blood," said Eugene.

"Why doesn't he want MINE?" yelled Baby Julia.

"He wants yours too," Eugene told her. "He wants everybody's." He waited a minute and looked around at all of us. "He likes blood," said Eugene.

Then Eugene took the knife with his left hand and jammed it into the pointing finger on his right hand.

"It's Frankenstein," said Gregory in a little voice.

"Shut up, Gregory," Eugene told him. "You're next." Gregory got whiter than ever.

We were all looking very hard at Eugene's hand. The drops of blood came up one after another, faster and faster out of the hole in Eugene's finger. They were like slithery black oil, awful in the candlelight.

"Hold out your hand, Gregory," said Eugene. He was not looking at him.

"No," Gregory said.

"Then Little Arthur says you have to get out of the club," said Eugene.

Gregory held out his hand and shut his eyes and Eugene cut it, and Gregory yelled way down in his throat, a yell that never got all the way out but stayed right there in his throat.

"I want to cut my own hand," said Baby Julia. "Lemme have that old knife." Her eyes were round and like two moons in her little baby face. She pulled it across the end of her thumb and made a long red line. Then she looked at it for a while before she remembered to yell. "Ow!" she yelled.

Sara Dell wouldn't let him do it at first but he grabbed her hand and did it anyway. Sara Dell never looked at her hand. She just looked at Eugene and her bottom lip went up and down like a doll with strings.

Robert said he would pick his scab, and he did, and I picked my own scab too so that the blood ran all down my leg. It made me want to laugh, only I didn't laugh at all.

We looked at each other across the candle. "Now," said Eugene, "we mix the blood. We mix it all up together and then we're a club." He rubbed his finger against Sara Dell's and I stuck my leg out and then everybody was putting their cuts on the blood of my leg and all our blood was mixing up together, black and runny on their hands and on my leg. Baby Julia was really bleeding a lot and she got some of it on her face, and Robert wanted some on his face too so Baby Julia rubbed her cut on it. Robert really looked funny. He had blood smack down the middle of his nose like an Indian chief. Then we were laughing and laughing and putting the blood all over our faces, even on Eugene's, until our faces were black and red and white in the candlelight.

"Whoo whoowhoo!" screamed Robert. He started jumping up and down like an Indian, hitting the ground hard with his feet, squishing and yelling in the mud. Gregory screamed too, in a voice higher than Robert's, and then we were all standing up and screaming and dancing by ourselves in the mud, and my leg kept bleeding and we kept putting more and more of the blood on our faces and dancing. Around and around we went. I got some of the blood in my mouth and it was sweet. I licked some more of it and yelled louder, and around and around we danced, jumping higher and higher. Then Gregory kicked over the candle.

For a while we stood there. Everything was black, and we were not dancing any more. I could hear them breathing but I couldn't see their faces, and all the air fell in on me and I thought I was dying. The air was not nice and smelling sweet any more. It was as heavy as rocks and far away in it there was more rain coming. I thought I couldn't breathe any more but I knew I was breathing.

"That's all," said Eugene. He talked from somewhere so close to me in the black that I jumped the other way and almost fell down in that slimy mud. "That's all for tonight," he said. "Meeting dismissed."

But nobody left or moved.

"Oh," said Eugene. "Little Arthur is pleased."

We left, going one by one down the path, and you couldn't see in front of you at all. The Tates' house up on the hill was big and black. It would have said awful things if it could talk, and I hated it and it scared me. I went right up to the bathroom when I got home, and took a bath first thing. The water turned a funny color from all the stuff that was in it. I ran some more water and took two baths.

The next afternoon it was still raining. Sara Dell's mother took us downtown and we went to the movies. I got two Butterfingers and a root beer. Sara Dell got one popcorn and one cherry smash. I wanted a peppermint patty too but I thought I'd wait because I knew I'd eat it right away if I went ahead and got it.

The movie was about these people in show business. They were walking along a street and they were all laughing, and wearing pretty clothes all the way through. They would walk along the street and then all of a sudden they would be singing and everybody they passed would sing too. The girls wore movie-star clothes and winked a lot. The thing I liked was the way everybody would start dancing. They were just walking along or having a picnic, or sitting in a hotel or something, and all of a sudden this music with drums came down out of the sky and everybody was dancing. The men jumped up high and clicked their heels. I thought that was so nice. I wish it happened to real people. Old Fred Astaire danced a dance by himself and he was real big. He was the only thing in the movie.

Sara Dell turned around. "I just can't stand it," she said. "I just can't stand it."

"What?" I asked her.

"FRED AS-TAIRE," she said. "Woo."

I laughed so hard my knees fell off the seat in front of me. Then Fred Astaire was kissing Ginger Rogers and their noses never got in the way. Their teeth didn't bump either. I couldn't figure out how they did that. I didn't know when they breathed or anything. I thought maybe they held their breaths but later on that night I found out for good and I was wrong.

After supper Baby Julia and I were outside catching lightning bugs. We put them all in a jar to make a big lightning bug lamp, and then when the jar was almost full Baby Julia's mama called her to come in and go to bed. I let all the lightning bugs go when she left even though I knew she would get mad. They looked like a flying star when they all flew out together.

The castle was dark when I went in. The Queen had gone away somewhere, and Elsie Mae was away up on the top floor in her own room, the Handmaiden's room. It was dark and I thought nobody was there until I heard the voices coming out of the living room. I stood in the doorway but I couldn't see anything. Then when my eyes got used to it I could see fine, so I sat right down on the floor where I was, to watch.

The Princess and Tom Cleveland were sitting on the sofa. At first I couldn't tell who it was because they were all squinched up together on the sofa, but pretty soon my eyes got to be just like cat eyes. He was kissing her. His head was turned sideways and hers was up and down so when they kissed each other their noses didn't hit. He kissed her for a very long time. I thought they could really swim because they could hold their breaths all that while, only then I found out. He went on kissing her and kissing her and pretty soon he got out of breath and started breathing very hard. Only he never stopped kissing her at the same time he was doing all that breathing. She was doing it too, and they got louder and louder until their breathing filled the whole room. The

Princess made a mmmmm sound in her throat at the same time.

By then they were almost lying flat on the couch, both of them, and he was still kissing her. I was still watching. It was dark in the room, like a movie, but it was better than any movie I ever saw. I thought maybe the Princess shouldn't lie down like that, though. For one thing, Tom Cleveland was so big he might squash her, and for another thing I thought it might be wrong. Only the Princess was older so she knew more about that stuff than I did, and besides Princesses have a lot of things they can do and nobody else. I knew that already. And I liked to watch them kiss each other. They kept moving around and changing the way they were doing it. If it was me, I thought, I would be tired by then; but they seemed to like it a lot. They kept right on.

My toe itched so I scratched it with very quiet fingers. The Princess and Tom Cleveland never looked where I was. The only place they looked was at each other, and they started really moving all around on that sofa, up and down and every way. They said a lot of things too soft for me to hear. Tom Cleveland talked right into the Princess' ear, so I never heard what he said at all. The Princess said "No" one or two times, and then she said "Please" and then she said "Why." I didn't even get sleepy sitting there.

They began batting around on the sofa like two crazy

people, and Tom Cleveland sounded the way Mrs. Abbott used to sound when she had asthma and we went to see her with boiled custard before she died. Then the Princess started making lots of noise, and things got more and more like the movies. She said all this stupid stuff. She said about how nothing ever worked out the way you thought it would. She said she loved a French guy. She said over and over how much she loved him and told Tom Cleveland over and over that she was sorry, but he didn't even know what love was. You wanted to kill yourself it was so bad, that's what it was like. I started to laugh right out loud but I didn't. She told Tom Cleveland he didn't have any idea. He pulled on her long yellow hair with his hands, sort of patted it like you do a dog, and said little things into her ear. I didn't think he was saying glug glug either, but I couldn't hear.

They rolled around a little, and the Princess was quiet. But after a while she started crying in that terrible way she had cried one night before. It was so bad it made you feel like throwing up, or like you wished she would throw up so it would be better. She started making all this noise and Tom Cleveland couldn't shut her up. Nobody could have shut her up. She was like the time the horn got stuck on Baby Julia's daddy's car, and it went on and on until the horn fixer man came.

"I worshipped her," said the Princess. "I really worshipped her." She talked so fast that you almost couldn't tell where a thing stopped off and the next one started. "One time when I was little we all went down the river to dinner and she wore a white dress. She had on that white dress and she ate lobster, and so I got lobster too but I couldn't handle it. I didn't know how to cut it up or anything and it got all over me. I remember the whole thing."

Tom Cleveland said quiet words into her ear and she yelled that she did not have too much to drink either. She said she guessed she was capable of knowing when she had too much to drink. She said she used to have wine with every meal in Paris. She had all these martinis on the boat coming back, for his information. She said, "Straight back from Paris to this, can you imagine?" She told Tom Cleveland to move his hand, please, that he was repulsing her. He said he didn't think he was. She said he didn't know anything and they both sat up on the sofa. Then the Princess started that crying again and leaning on him. I knew she was really slopping up his shirt but it was too dark to see it.

"Why can't you ever love anybody?" she said, only she didn't want anybody to answer her. "Cynical people are great. It's the only way to be. I'd love to be cynical, I'm going to practice it every day. When somebody says good morning I'll say sure, and then I'll boo and hiss. Only that isn't very cynical at all." She was crying again, and she talked faster and faster and higher in her throat. "See, I can't even do it. Those people must have started when they were babies. I bet they thought their creamed spinach was B-grade the whole time. That's what you have to do, you have to start early and build up your defenses. Or else you don't have any. You're a good guy, Tom Cleveland, but you think I'm drunk."

I had to put my hand on my mouth to keep laughs from coming out. My feet had gone to sleep and I had the best pins and needles in them. They tickled.

He patted her head and the Princess let out all her breath in a big sigh. I thought everything was over but she got mad another time. "Quit *stroking* my hair," she said. "Just don't *stroke* me. Oh, you'll be a real pillar, Tom. I can see your mother now. She'll be so proud. She'll say there he is, that's my son Tom, he's been so successful, look at him, he's such a pillar of the community. She'll be smiling and everything." The way the Princess said that, I couldn't tell if she thought Tom's mother should smile or not. It was a funny voice.

Tom Cleveland kissed her again and their mouths made a little splop-splop noise. He said everything would be all right. They mushed around some more. I was getting sleepy all over, besides my feet.

The Princess said she was sorry, Tom, he was a great guy but she hated him now. She said he knew all this stuff now and so she had to hate him. She said he understood that, didn't he? Tom Cleveland said, "My God, Betty, don't be so typical."

The Princess told him maybe he should leave now, anyway. Maybe she would see him tomorrow. Tom Cleveland got up and put on the clothes which he had had off, and I went on my hands and knees like a crawdad behind a big chair. The Princess turned on the light in the hall. Her hair was all messed up. It was all over everywhere, and her face was very red, but she was still pretty.

Tom Cleveland opened the door and didn't say a word. "Tom," the Princess said to his back in a little voice, "I love you."

I just about died.

"You probably do," said Tom Cleveland. "Good night."

He went out the door without turning around.

The Princess stood still for a minute and chewed on her long yellow hair, then she yelled, "Just a minute. Wait a minute please." She didn't have any shoes on but she ran out the door. I never saw what they did next, but I think the Princess was going to kiss him. That's the way her face looked. I ran zoom up the stairs while she was outside. When I thought about the way they had been mushing and all, it made me feel funny around my legs.

I brushed my teeth upstairs with pink toothpaste. My whole mouth got pink and foamy, like a mad dog. The Princess came up the stairs and went into her room. One of my back pink teeth started woggling around in my mouth. When I punched it with my finger it was almost ready to come out, so I went down the stairs to get an apple. One bite and it came right out. I took the tooth back upstairs with me and put it under the pillow for the Good Fairy, and then I got into bed and kissed John Doe good night.

The door opened all of a sudden and it was the Queen. She came in the door like wind, swishing around in her dress. "Susan?" said the Queen. "Susan dear, are you asleep?"

"No," I said.

"Oh, Susan," said the Queen. She whooshed over to me and sat on the bed, and put her arms around me and John Doe and kissed the top of my head. I opened my eyes but I couldn't see anything. There was all this net stuff in my eyes, and all I could smell was summer. The light from the door came into the room in a bright yellow road and when I moved my face I could see it landing on my bed.

The Queen kissed the top of my head again. I stayed on the pillow without moving, the light hitting my eyes. I couldn't see her face. She said, "I love you, Susan. You know that, don't you?" and her voice didn't sound much like a bird or a piano any more.

"Yeah," I told her. I did know it too, right then. I am loved by the Queen, I thought. I mean beloved. She stood up and kissed her hand at me. Then she left fast like she had come, shutting the door, and the yellow light was gone from my bed. A Queen loves me, I thought. I am loved by a Queen. I had that, and Daddy's pictures, and a lot of secrets, and a tooth under my pillow. I put my hand under the pillow and it was right there. I could hold it with my fingers.

But I didn't hold it. I let go so the Good Fairy could take it and leave me money there instead. Of course, by that time I didn't really believe in the Good Fairy any more. I was so old I knew better. When I was little I thought that the Good Fairy really brought the money and took the tooth. Then when I got big I found out that fairies don't have any quarters, that all they have is fairy money. So the Good Fairy tells a person, and the person puts the money. That's the way it really works. I wondered what time she would come, late at night or very soon, and if she would fly or walk.

The next club meeting was in the afternoon, and for one time it was sunny. I said, "I thought all our club meetings were at night. I thought this was a night club," and Eugene said no, if Little Arthur wanted to meet in the afternoons, we would meet in the afternoons. Whatever Little Arthur wanted to do, he said, and he was right. Little Arthur was the President. So we met that afternoon, and it was hot and sunny.

"Besides, you can't call it a night club," Eugene said. "Night clubs are in cities and have bands." Sara Dell laughed. I laughed too. I thought it was probably the only funny thing old Eugene would ever say and I had better laugh while I could.

The night before the meeting it had rained, so little white clouds came up from all the bushes and from the leaves where the sun was hot on them. The air was hot and wet and stuck to the inside of my nose. My face was sticky all over, like it wanted to sweat but couldn't. I looked under Sara Dell's arms to see if she was sweating while we walked along the path. One day she was but that day she wasn't. Only big people do that but Sara Dell did it too. That and her hair, long like it was, were two reasons I liked old Sara Dell. I tried to sweat under my arms too, but I couldn't do it, or make my hair grow long like hers either.

Mrs. Tate was out in her rosebushes when we walked up the path. We could see her, far away and bent over with her back turned. We had to scrunch over and go quiet so that she wouldn't hear us or see us. Mrs. Tate was pulling weeds. We scrunched all the way to the clubhouse through the things that were not really flowers or weeds either, but in between, all the hot growing things that were high along the path.

The clubhouse was hot. It was misty hot from the rain and then the sunlight, squishy wet where we sat.

"Hey!" yelled Baby Julia.

"Shut up," said everybody.

"Hey," said Baby Julia, not as loud, "where's old Eugene and Little Arthur?"

I thought maybe they were at the back of the whole club, coming up the path behind us, but they were not.

"I want Little Arthur," yelled Baby Julia. "Where is he, anyway?"

"I thought he was coming," said Sara Dell. "I thought he was right behind us."

"Who needs old Eugene, anyway?" Robert said. He didn't say Little Arthur, though. "Who needs him anyway is what I'd like to know. I'm going to start the meeting because I'm the biggest Vice-President."

"I'm a Vice-President too," said Gregory, tying the strings on his tennis shoes.

"I'm bigger than you are," I said.

"Shut up," Robert told everybody. His hair was too long and it fell into one eye. "You're a girl. I'm the oldest Vice-President who is the biggest boy. See? MEETING IS STARTED!" he yelled.

"You don't even know how to do it right," Gregory said.

"I won't meet at the meeting if Little Arthur doesn't come," said Baby Julia. "I LOVE Little Arthur."

"I think you say 'attention,' " Sara Dell said to Robert. "But don't."

"Meeting is started," Robert hollered. His cheeks were as red as doll cheeks and his hair was all over his eyes.

"It is not," Eugene said quietly. He and Little Arthur had come from noplace, out of the sticky white day into the clubhouse, with no noise, not one sound. "Little Arthur will speak to you later, Robert," he said. He didn't look at Robert. It was hot in the clubhouse.

"Goody," said Baby Julia. "I bet he gives you hell," she said to Robert.

"Baby Julia!" yelled Sara Dell. I would have laughed if it wasn't a meeting. Baby Julia was so fat and cute, and saying hell like that. It was funny.

Eugene had a book in his hand. It was a green leather book, very tall and skinny, that looked old and not for kids. He was holding it so tight that the white bones showed in his hand. He and Little Arthur sat down and we sat down too, in the circle like always. Robert looked funny. "Meeting is called to order," Eugene said in that voice. Before this summer I didn't even know I had hair on the back of my neck. I thought it was just skin there. Only that summer I found out about the hair because at club meetings it always moved up and down, like bugs on the back of my neck.

Eugene put the green book on his knees and we looked at it for a long time. "Little Arthur is angry with Robert," he said. "But the club meeting shall continue. Little Arthur has called this club meeting in the daytime so that everyone can see. Little Arthur wants everyone to see this book." I bet it was because Little Arthur and Eugene took the book without telling, while his aunt was away. But I didn't say it. I looked at the book.

It was a green book, very old, made for grown people who had been away to school. There were faraway markings on the front cover and gold on the sides of the pages. "This book," Eugene said, "is an art book."

Baby Julia ate a piece of grass that she had gotten on the way, and looked out at the flowers and bushes. "Little Arthur is interested in art," Eugene said loud, and she looked again at the green book. "This is a special kind of art. This book is full of statues and paintings and they are quite beautiful. We will look at them now."

He opened the book to the first page and there was a

picture of a man with no clothes on. He had a little basket on his head and he was leaning sideways. That basket was cute and I smiled. But then Eugene said, "Little Arthur says this is serious. Little Arthur says that nobody should smile." He put his finger where the man with the basket on his head went to the bathroom. "What is that?" he asked. It was the voice that teachers use, when they already know the answer but want to make you tell them anyway.

"Listen here," said Sara Dell, and then she shut up. She was sweating under the arms now and there was a fly on her foot, but she let it stay there.

"It's a DOO-LOLLY!" yelled Baby Julia. "My daddy has one."

"It is not," said Eugene. It's a penis."

"What?" said Sara Dell. "A what?" She leaned forward and her hair was long on her shoulders. Her eyes were open very wide.

"I guess I do so know what it is," said Baby Julia. "It's a doo-lolly. Doo-lolly, doo-lolly, doo-lolly. Ha."

"Little Arthur wants everybody to know about art," Eugene told us. "This is a penis. Say that after me, Baby Julia. Penis."

"Penis," she said, and giggled.

"Now we will go around the circle," Eugene said, "and everybody will touch the penis in the book and say it. All right, Robert."

"Old penis," said Robert, and punched it with a finger. His finger was dirty.

We all did it, and it got hotter in the clubhouse. When it was over Baby Julia said, "Ask Little Arthur if I can do it again. I want to do it again. I'm the nurse."

Eugene said that Little Arthur had something else next. He turned over some pages in the art book, going very fast by two old people, and a house and some flowers and a woman with a big dress in a swing, and got to a fat girl lying on the grass and looking straight up out of that green art book. When the art book was flat she looked at the top of the clubhouse. She was so fat there were lumps in her all over and she was in color. A hill was behind her, and pink flowers were messed up with her hair. "Breast," said Eugene. He poked at it with his finger. It was red and pointy and fat. When he punched it with his finger I jumped a mile, and all the bugs crawled together up the back of my neck and down again. Those bugs were awful.

I put my finger on her and said it, and everybody did. She sat on the page and looked at the top of the clubhouse while we did it. She didn't even care. Robert jabbed at it harder than anybody else and said it louder, and then I thought her eyes blinked but they didn't of course because she wasn't anything but a fat girl in a skinny green art book. When we had all touched her we didn't look at each other. I thought about how it would be to be punched there, not now but later when I got fat. When I got beauty. I didn't even want to get beauty if I would get punched. What's the good of that, I thought, to get beauty and even be in a green book, if people punch at you, I thought. My legs felt funny again and I thought about the Princess and Tom Cleveland on that sofa. And Ginger Rogers in the movie. I thought Ginger Rogers had never been punched.

Also in the art book was a black and white picture, two black people made out of rock who were hugging and kissing on each other without wearing any clothes.

"They're necking," said Sara Dell.

"Little Arthur says that's the way you start," Eugene said, "before you make a baby." I didn't know about making a baby and I didn't ask either. I looked at Robert and he was grinning. A big wide grin that went all over him and was not like the grin he usually did. The black people were all squished into each other, and his muscles showed strong under the thick black skin. Some way, the muscles were fine. The muscles made everything all right, and only Robert grinning made it not nice.

"Before they fuck that's what they do," Eugene told us.

"Oh," I said. I had not ever heard that before but I would put it away in my mind to keep for good. Fuck, I thought. The black people were twisting on the page and the clubhouse was hot.

"Meeting is adjourned," Eugene said. "Little Arthur is pleased."

"That was a fun meeting," Baby Julia said to Eugene. "I liked it," she said to Little Arthur. "Come on," she said to me, and we left going down the path with Sara Dell right behind and the sweat under her arms. Only Robert stayed behind because Little Arthur wanted to talk to him. I was glad Little Arthur didn't want to talk to me.

"Well," said Sara Dell. That was all she said for a while.

A bee sat on my hand and then flew away. They don't ever sting me.

"What about that," I said. "I guess everybody does like that before babies are born."

"Not black," said Baby Julia.

"No," Sara Dell said, "but just think."

"What about Ginger Rogers and Fred Astaire," I said.

"King Edward and Mrs. Simpson," Sara Dell said.

"President Roosevelt and Mrs. Roosevelt."

"Old Mr. Tate and Mrs. Tate," Sara Dell said and we laughed and laughed.

"Our mamas and our daddies," Baby Julia yelled. We walked on down the path.

"When I was little," Baby Julia said, and she was still little, "I thought babies came under cabbage leaves."

"That's only in Germany," Sara Dell said. "In America you fuck."

"Yeah, I know." I felt very old. "If they came under cabbage leaves all the time, Baby Julia, nobody in cities could get them. Not in America anyway. In America you pick them up at the hospital." I thought about going into the Piggly Wiggly, into the orange and lettuce part of the market, and buying some tomatoes and a baby. But I knew babies came from God. After you fucked, I guessed. You prayed and then you got one if you were married.

It was almost time for supper and everybody's daddies were coming home. We could look from where we were and see them. I felt funny, like the bushes all around were mountains. I was standing in the middle of the mountains just before I found a secret place, and the dogs were looking at me from behind the trees. Only they didn't bark. Then I was in the garden of the palace and Frank was in the flowers.

I wished I had that green book for my very own and then I was glad I didn't. I wished too we would have hot dogs for supper but I knew we never had them. We always had more dressy things.

The next day the Princess and the Queen were fighting, or anyway the Princess was fighting and the Queen was listening, and Elsie Mae was frying chicken. The frying and fighting spread out until it was a little bit all over the house, and I went outside to the dogbushes. Royalty acts like that sometimes, and younger royalty acts worse than older royalty. Like the Queen and the Princess. But you get used to Queens and Princesses and things. Only you can't ever get too used to them. If you could get too used to them they wouldn't be royal, but you can't ever do it anyway.

I sat under my best dogbush. First I felt like a woman of the world and then I felt like I was two. My head was funny this summer. It was too little for all the things I was putting into it and it felt tight all the time. It was a special summer head.

Two dogbush flowers were dead in front of me so I picked them up and held them in my hands for a long time. They weren't pink any more, they were brown and floppy and dead in my hands. After I had looked at them I made a little grave in the dirt and put them there. I covered them up and said the blessing. Everything that dies ought to get buried. Like trees, and flowers, and birds, and little mice. People too. Sometimes they burn people when they die but that isn't right. Only God gets to burn you, that oldest God with all the hair, and then just if you're bad. But you ought to get your own grave first like the dogbush flowers. I thought maybe they had yelled when they died, and I couldn't hear them because my ears were human ears.

Maybe all the grass was yelling right then, when Frank mowed it with the lawn mower; maybe it was yelling help in a million awful voices and I couldn't hear. Maybe the tree hurt when the wind blew it, and cried like it was sick. I put dirt all around the grave. I wouldn't mind it too bad to be under the earth, I thought. If I was under the earth I would know everything in the world, and I wouldn't mind it at all.

I thought about the Good Fairy tooth next because that was what I went out there to think about. I had put it under my pillow and didn't tell, because I wanted to buy Elsie Mae a big Butterfinger with the quarter and have a surprise Butterfinger party with it. So I didn't tell, and the Good Fairy didn't come. I thought maybe she had a day off or was too busy. So the next night I had put it there again, right like it should be, and when I woke up I looked under my pillow first thing and it was still there with a little bit of blood on the ends.

I took it and showed it to Elsie Mae and asked her what was the matter with the tooth.

"It's not in your head, that's what," said little old Elsie Mae. She thought it was a game and laughed. "Hee, hee, hee. That just come out?"

"No," I said. I put it in my pocket and went out the door.

"You better put that under your pillow tonight,"

Elsie Mae said to my back. "You better make sure it's under there and the Good Fairy'll bring you something nice." She was washing dishes. They hit against each other and sounded nice in the sink.

"I did that already," I told her.

"And the Good Fairy she didn't come with a nice little something?"

"She's off," I said.

"Well, I'll tell her," Elsie Mae said, her little feet shining like the bubbles in the sink. "You go put it under there tonight and I'll tell her proper. Then you look under your pillow and see what you see."

I put it under the pillow again, and when I got up a pretty, round quarter was there. Only it wasn't any good, it wasn't the same thing like if she had come that first night. I thought, what if she didn't come at all and Elsie Mae did it, but I never asked Elsie Mae. I put the quarter in my white socks and left it. I didn't want to get a Butterfinger or have a Butterfinger party anymore. All of a sudden I thought that Butterfingers were stupid; but I didn't want to think that and it made me mad.

I couldn't figure out what was the matter with the Good Fairy and what made her act that way. Nothing worked any more like it ought to. The Good Fairy was supposed to tell a human and then the human put the money. Only the way it worked this time, a human told a human and then that human put the money. I couldn't see where the Good Fairy came into it at all. Everything was human. I thought for a long time not very nice things about the Good Fairy, like I wished she would break a wing. Then I thought maybe she never was a good fairy at all, maybe she never was anything, but I didn't want to think that and I pushed it out of my head with a finger. I decided she had flu.

Frank went up and down, up and down with his lawn mower. He made me feel good, because I knew whatever happened old Frank would be right there taking care of the yard. He wasn't like the Good Fairy. He was a part of the yard. He never looked up but he couldn't see me if he did, for the dogbushes. Up and down and up and down. I thought about the morning he was drunk and he went around and around. I liked both ways the same because it was just old Frank. He could go either way he wanted as long as he did it in our yard. I liked having him there. I wished I was drunk. I would sing "Amazing Grace" like Frank and feel good in my summer head. How sweet the sound of amazing grace. The lawn mower sounded like a long sneeze. It went on and on, up and down, in little cutting roads.

You could smell the rain in the air, but it smelled far away and I could tell it wouldn't come before night, when I was sleeping. Elsie Mae stuck her head out the

door and put it back in, and up on the hill I could see
the Tates' house. The Princess and Tom Cleveland went
away in a car with tennis rackets, and Gregory's cat
walked slowly across the back yards. He walked by the
swings and I thought about how high I used to swing
in them and then I would bail out. I would be flying
for a while, then glad when I hit grass. That's what
summers were like before, I thought. But I wasn't sure.
Nothing is real unless it is happening to you. I thought
how we used to swing and bail out, and Sara Dell and I
had the biggest fight in the neighborhood one year over
a paper doll that was really mine, and Gregory kept
wanting to play paper dolls with us but we never let
him because he was a boy. One time we called him sissy
and he cried and I cried too.

Last summer one time Sara Dell and I both had dimes
to walk to the Esso station and buy Popsicles with. We
walked along and she dropped hers, not on the ground
but in the cattle guard at the end of Robert's driveway.
We reached down with our fingers but we couldn't
find it. Sara Dell stuck her head there between the bars
and all you could see was her neck and her rear end in
shorts, stuck straight up. Sara Dell didn't have a head.
I laughed and laughed, and Sara Dell laughed too down
in the cattle guard. I stuck my head in. Then we
couldn't turn our heads and we couldn't find the dime
and we couldn't pull our heads out because they were

stuck in the cattle guard. We laughed until they came and bent the bars and got our heads out. Then Sara Dell's mama gave us two more dimes and we got ice-cream sandwiches. That was the way last summer was, I thought. I couldn't think of everything we did.

Gregory and Robert were throwing a football at each other then and I could just see a little bit of them from the dogbushes where I was. It was the best hiding place I knew. I would hide there in a game, like hide-and-seek, because I didn't want anybody to find the hiding place and Robert might. He was quick. He threw that football harder than Gregory, and he never missed catching it. I wondered what he and Little Arthur had said. When Robert had grinned that way he had been awful. He was still Robert but he was awful. I wondered if Tom Cleveland was grinning like that in the dark on the sofa, and maybe Fred Astaire when he looked at Ginger and you saw him from the back and couldn't see his face.

My summer head was too tight. Frank went up and down, up and down, and made me happy. It was pretty hot and I bet he had sweat under his arms like Sara Dell. The Queen never did, of course. Queens don't sweat. A bee came into the dogbushes with me.

I got up and went out the back way to the wading house. In the wading house it was quiet and cooler than in the dogbushes. The water was clear where I stood.

It ran away past my feet and I thought about where it was going. Two little fishes swam next to the bank with their mama fish. She was showing them things in the water, and it made me want to cry. But I couldn't because my head was too full.

When you're a baby, like Baby Julia, nothing pushes or squiggles inside your head. You've got a very full head but it's all right, because all babies know so much. They know everything in the whole world. That's why they crawl, because they know so much they can't take it all around with them. It's too heavy and they are too small. When you get older you forget, and the more you forget, the better you can walk. That's what is the matter with my summer head, I thought. I never forgot enough and I was putting new stuff in that there wasn't any room for.

Like Eugene. And the art book. And mostly Little Arthur. I wished I knew Little Arthur better, and his gun, and his hat and everything. I wished I could spend long, long times talking to Little Arthur but not talking to Eugene too. I still remembered the first day Eugene came to stay with Mrs. Parks and the way he threw the rock at that little mouse. Eugene was awful and his eyes were the worst part. Even in the dark at club meetings you could see those eyes. I didn't know why Little Arthur would want to stay with somebody who had eyes like that. He would rather stay with me if he knew me better.

The mama fish went between my feet while the baby fish stayed by the bank. I guessed they hadn't learned to do that yet, go between people's feet. I thought about the Queen and how she was bright and quicker even than the mama fish. Then I thought about Little Arthur some more, and that green art book, and Little Arthur and the Queen got all junked up together in my summer head. But the Queen loved me. She had said so, that night when the light was a yellow road across my bed. She had kissed my head. I made the water muddy with my feet and the fish ran away. The Queen really loved me, Susan, and I loved the Queen and Little Arthur both.

In the sky it thundered. I wished it wouldn't rain any more. I was getting sick of the rain. I didn't think it rained last summer but I couldn't remember. Last summer Little Arthur wasn't around, though, or Eugene. The day that I first saw Eugene was the day summer started, and you have to finish a summer the way it starts.

One day I came in from the rain all nice and wet, and went to drip in the kitchen. Elsie Mae was banging all around not saying a word, which was a funny way for her to act. After I dripped for a little while I went into the den.

The Princess and the Queen were there and I was wet. They sat across the room from each other. The Queen was looking at a magazine and the Princess was looking out the window, and the air in the room was jumpy and stiff like it is before a big storm outside. You could tell that something bad had happened already or was going to.

In the Queen's magazine were lots of skinny girls with black eyes, wearing pretty clothes. She turned them over one by one very fast, so that the pages went click, click, click. She didn't like them very much. But then she was prettier, the Queen, than all those skinny girls rolled up together. She wore a red dress, the kind of red that is middle between purple and red, and her lips were red like her dress. That day her foot tapped, little short taps on the floor where the rug wasn't, and one hand kept flying up to her hair. She was beautiful. The Queen always sat so that she fitted right into whatever she sat in, even if it was straight and not curvy, she always fitted right into it like she lived there. That's one way you can spot a Queen. She was through with the magazine and she put it down hard on the little table. It went snap when it hit.

"I think it's the most ridiculous thing I ever heard of," she said.

The Princess looked out the window and pulled at her long yellow hair. Her face was away from me.

"Hi, Susan," she said. "How's the rain?"

"It's pretty good," I said. "It's just like bath water."

"Susan," the Queen said, louder, and laughed. "You're soaked clear through. Go upstairs this minute and put on some dry clothes." She laughed her sunny laugh when she looked at me.

"I will in just a minute," I said. "I already dripped in the kitchen."

"I'm pinned to Tom Cleveland now," Betty said. I saw that she was talking to me and I jumped. "I got pinned last night." The Princess' eyes were like grape popsicles.

I said, "Oh." I didn't know what else to say. The Princess wanted me to say something, but I didn't know what it was.

"Come over here and look at my pin," the Princess said. I went over and looked at it. My feet left little wet places behind me on the rug everywhere I went. I felt kind of funny about looking, because she had it pinned right on the pointy place. It was a pretty pin, gold with lots of sparkle.

"I like it," I said. "It's a pretty pin."

"Oh, but you don't know what it means, Susan," the Queen said. She lit a cigarette and I could smell the match very strong. "It means your sister is almost engaged." I looked at the Princess and the Princess looked out the window. "Yes, Betty is almost engaged now. Our little Betty. To wonderful Tom Cleveland. You like Tom Cleveland, don't you?"

"Sure," I said. Now the Queen wanted me to say something but I didn't know what it was either. I felt all tied up.

"Oh, Tom Cleveland is marvelous," said the Queen. She was the only one I ever knew who used that word. "We all like Tom. He's such a fine, solid, boring citizen. Like a rock, and I quote."

"I thought he went glug glug glug," I said. I didn't know what was going on and I was trying to help.

That made the Princess mad. "He does not," she said loud.

"Aren't women fickle?" the Queen asked nobody. "I suppose everyone has a right to change her mind, however. Betty can't go out with anyone except Tom now," she said. They both looked at me.

"She doesn't anyway," I said.

"That's exactly right, she doesn't," the Queen said. "And when I was your age, dear," she said to the Princess, "you couldn't count the number of men underfoot."

"Oh, I'm sure," the Princess said in an ugly voice.

"You just don't know what you're missing," the Queen told her. "You could do a lot better."

"What do you mean, better?" the Princess said. "You mean with more money or something? Look, I know the kind of man you would like for me to marry— mainly for your own reasons—but I just don't think I want to any more. I can't help it. If you had all these great guys around you all the time when you were young, why didn't you marry one?"

Both of them sat up straight and it was like I wasn't even there any more.

"Betty," the Queen said, "it's for your own good. You can see what happens. There are a lot of things you don't know. You're still very young, you know."

"Sure," Betty said. She sounded like she didn't believe a word.

"All marriages aren't made in a church," the Queen said, speaking in a tiny voice and leaning across the room at the Princess. "Sometimes everything isn't all roses. Sometimes people have to get married."

"Jesus," said the Princess. "You sound like Dorothy Dix. That's so trite. Besides, I've known about that for years. At least I can count."

"Hey," I said. "Why do people have to get married?"

They jumped. The Queen smiled at me, one of the most beautiful smiles she ever smiled. "Just because they love each other," she said. "Oh, *look* what you've done to the rug! Susan, go upstairs this minute and put on some dry clothes."

There was a dark place going out all around my feet. I felt like it would go all over the whole room and the whole house unless I moved my feet quick. I felt, too, all of a sudden, like Little Arthur was in the house. I knew he was. I thought that right then he was upstairs sitting on my bed.

I went upstairs the back way, two at a time. My heart went bump all the way. When I went into my room, Little Arthur was not there but the air was moving and I knew that he had just left. He had been sitting on the end of my bed. I was sorry I was too late, but I thought that he would come again.

For the next few days the Princess and the Queen were just like a movie in our house. I always came in at that part before all of a sudden everybody in the movie stops in the middle of the street and starts singing a big loud song. It was never the singing, only the part before. And outside, it was raining.

I thought about love a lot and I couldn't figure anything out. There are about a zillion things that you call love, and none of them are like each other at all. I loved John Doe. The black man in the art book loved the black woman. The Queen loved me. God loved the world. I loved Little Arthur. Eugene loved Little Arthur and I didn't love Eugene, but I loved Little Arthur too. It was all different. I thought that if any old boy ever told me he loved me I had better ask him which way, quick, before anything else happened.

One day I talked about it to Elsie Mae. I was helping her pull strings off beans in the kitchen.

"Elsie Mae," I said, "have you ever been in love?"

"I reckon," said Elsie Mae. "What you want to know for?"

"I just do," I said. "I want to know, is all. Tell me about when you were in love."

"I don't know if I can remember right," said Elsie Mae. "It was a mighty long time ago." She rocked and I waited. I was glad I thought of asking Elsie Mae. She was smart, maybe not about books but about other things. I was the only one in the castle who knew how smart Elsie Mae was. Even the Queen didn't know and thought Elsie Mae was pretty dumb, because one time at a dinner party I heard her tell all the members of the Court about the first time Elsie Mae came to the castle, back before I was born. The phone rang and the Queen was outside and called to Elsie Mae to answer it, please, and since there are three phones in the castle, Elsie Mae came running out and asked which one did the Queen want her to answer. The Queen didn't know how smart Elsie Mae was at all, because she told that out loud at the party to the members of the Court.

"I was in love lots," said Elsie Mae, "but two times mainly."

"I didn't think you got married," I said. I sat up on the kitchen floor straight.

"Oh, law," said Elsie Mae. "You don't have to marry somebody just because of you love them. And you don't have to love somebody just because of you marry them."

"You don't?" I laid my back flat on the floor and put my feet up on the refrigerator so all the blood would go to my head and I could think better. "I thought you did." From where I was I could see Elsie Mae's light-blue feet and her legs were as thin as little sticks above them.

"Well, you don't," she said. "There isn't no rhyme or no reason to the thing at all. You just can't ever tell." She rocked back and shut her little glittery eyes. "The first time I was in love I wasn't but seventeen. That don't make a bit of difference either, how young you are or how old. Boy from someplace away come in to work on the road and I saw him out there, swinging a big hammer and breaking rocks and singing just as loud the whole time. He was a right fine sight. Those rocks went ever which way when he hit them with that hammer. He was a mighty strong young boy." Elsie Mae grinned at the kitchen clock which said three.

"So one night they was a county fair. It was a Saturday night and I put on my new dress and says, 'Pappy, I'm going to the fair,' and I guess I'm looking right determined because he says, 'Well go on then, if you're that much of a mind to,' and I went. They was rides, and candy apples, and horses racing, and about a million people. I didn't find him till ten o'clock."

"Find who?" I asked her.

"That boy."

"What boy? You mean the boy with the hammer?"

"Yep," said Elsie Mae. "Hee, hee, hee. He was shooting ducks. There was this little machine and ever time a duck would pop up he would shoot it and it would fall over. So I walked right up and I says, 'I want a Teddy bear,' and he shot some more ducks and got me one."

"But you didn't know him," I said.

Elsie Mae was still smiling at the clock. "I got that Teddy bear and he went right on shooting ducks and after a while we had the biggest pile of Teddy bears you ever saw. I couldn't hold them all and they were piled up all around us in the sawdust. He kept shooting and every time he pulled the trigger another duck would fall over dead. Finally we got so many Teddy bears that everybody was buying them off of us, and I was taking in the money. We had us quite a considerable crowd gathered around to watch that boy shoot ducks."

I thought about Elsie Mae standing in the County Fair with Teddy bears all around her, but it was a hard thing to think of. I was used to her being in the kitchen of the castle so it was hard. "What happened then?" I said.

"Well, after a while they done ran out of Teddy bears. The last one was green as I remember, and after that there wasn't any more left."

"How'd you get all those Teddy bears home?" I asked her.

"Law, honey, we didn't take all those Teddy bears home. What would I ever do with all them Teddy bears. We just left them laying where they was and walked off and took us a ride on the Ferris wheel and ate two things of cotton candy apiece. Then I got sick, from that cotton candy I reckon, so I went home."

I felt like she hadn't played fair to finish it off so quick like that. "What happened to him?" I asked. "What happened to the boy that shot the ducks?"

"We went off to Memphis," she said. "And one night I ate turtle soup in a restaurant."

I thought turtle soup would be awful but she was smiling. "How long did you stay in Memphis?"

"Right long," she said. "I forget. Then I come home."

"What'd you come home for, if you liked it up there so much? I mean the turtle soup and all."

"I don't know. I missed Pappy and Ella Mae," she said. Ella Mae was Elsie Mae's sister only they weren't twins like you would think because of the name. She had told me about Ella Mae lots before. "I reckon I just come home," she said.

I asked her about when else she was in love.

"It was some years after that. This man he come to stay at my house and I was in love with him, I reckon. He was a fine man."

"He came to stay at your house," I said. "What did he come to stay at your house for? I thought your Pappy and Ella Mae were there."

"They was there too."

"Well, what did he come for then?" I said.

"He just came." Elsie Mae rocked. "Lawd, could that man eat! That man could eat more than anybody I ever saw in my life. And drink more too. But he sure could eat. If you wanted anything yourself you just about had to grab it and run because he ate so fast. Then when he was through with what he had on his plate, he would eat yours if you didn't watch out. Used to make me right tired to watch that man eat."

"What was his name?" I asked, but she didn't say.

She said, "One day the Reverend Mr. Jenkins was coming in for dinner and we had to make that man eat out on the back porch. We knew what would of happened if he had sat at the table. He would of eaten all the Reverend's food quicker than scat because the Reverend he ate mighty slow indeed. So we had to put this man out back where he couldn't get at the Reverend's food."

"What made him eat so much?" The more I thought about that man the more I liked him.

"Hungry," said Elsie Mae.

She rocked awhile and told me some more about how much he ate. There was one time at a church picnic and one time at a social and one time right after Pappy killed the hog.

I asked her whatever happened to him.

"He went away," said Elsie Mae.

"Just like that?" I said. "He never came back or anything, he just went away?"

"He went away," she said again. It didn't seem to make her sad at all.

I lay back on the floor to think about things. The rain was outside the window and Elsie Mae rocked with the pan of beans on her knees.

"I thought you loved somebody because they were good," I said, "or handsome or something."

"You thinks what you thinks," said Elsie Mae. "I ain't telling you what to think."

"Then if that isn't why, why is it? Is it because of the way somebody can shoot ducks or how much he can eat? Is that why?"

"They is a lot of reasons," Elsie Mae said. "I reckon those is as good as any."

The Princess stood in the kitchen door in a raincoat. "Susan," she said, "come on. I want you to ride down to the drugstore with me." She looked like I had to go so I went.

"You shouldn't spend so much time with Elsie Mae," the Princess said, driving the car with the windshield wipers going. "She's so old she's half crazy. Besides, it's not a good idea to spend so much time with the help."

I was sitting out in the dogbushes, not doing anything at all. I was trying to think or move so that I could be a part of the dogbushes and then I'd know how they thought and moved. Only that day I had trouble being a dogbush. There was something I knew I wanted to do, and after a while I thought of it. I got up and went in to the castle.

"Hey Elsie Mae," I yelled.

"What you want," she yelled from the kitchen.

"Nothing," I yelled back.

I went to the stairs. "Mother," I called, and nobody answered. I didn't think the Queen would be in her chambers, not really, but I thought I would find out for sure. The Princess was away somewhere with Tom Cleveland. I had seen them leave.

I sat down a minute because things are always better if you wait. Like ice cream gets better the more you mash it up. Then I went downstairs to the basement, to Daddy's workshop. I went by the little road through the junk, very slow to make the waiting longer. I touched the washing machine with a finger. It was as clean and as nice as it looked. I pushed open the door to the workshop and it was light. Bright light came in from the high little window, and like before there was nothing in the room except that long flat table.

I opened the closet door next, with my stomach doing butterflies because I couldn't wait. They were all there like I knew they would be. I put them one by one on the gray table and when that was full I put them one by one on the floor. It took me a long time because I looked at every one as I did it.

My summer head went back to the way it was before, for a little while. I thought if I looked at those pictures long enough I would know all the nice things there are to know.

Sun came in and made the paint shine back at it. It was prettiest where the paint was thick and swirly. There the sunlight had to go in circles to catch up.

One picture was new since the last time. The more I looked at that one, the more I wasn't sure if I liked it or not. It was pretty, but I didn't know. It was like lime sherbert. You know you don't like it very much and you don't really want to eat it, but it's so light green that you go ahead and eat it anyway. This picture was like that. It made me look at it for a long time but I didn't want to very much because it made my chest hurt too. I think it looked like it was breathing hard. The picture was a face, the face of the Queen. It didn't look like the Queen too much, only it was. The whole back of the picture was black and the face grew out of that blackness until you knew the white part of the face wasn't really white but only lighter black. The mouth was too big. It opened and opened until it almost had everything else inside it, all the other pictures and me too. The eyes of that picture were way back in its head. You could almost see them but not quite, and you were glad that you couldn't. The main thing was the mouth, though. It went on and on forever. I knew it was awful but it was beautiful too. That messed me up because how can something be beautiful and awful at the same time?

I thought I had looked at the pictures long enough. I stuck them away like they were before. The last one I looked at for a while to make me feel good. It was one I had liked before, a field of grass with a big fat cow. The cow was fat and brown and she didn't care what happened. I liked her a lot. Then I shut the little door.

My chest was still funny and tight so I played Charlie McCarthy and Edgar Bergen all by myself until it quit.

The way I played it was to look like Charlie McCarthy but sound like Edgar Bergen, and jerk my hands like wood. Gregory and I used to play it together some, except with Gregory it wasn't any fun. He always wanted to be Edgar and not Charlie, and you are supposed to take turns being Edgar and Charlie when you play.

The telephone rang upstairs in the living room and I ran all the way up there. I didn't know why but I thought it might be for me. But it wasn't, it was only the Baron calling the Queen.

"She's not here," I said. "I don't know where she is." I didn't know how I knew it was the Baron either but I knew. Then I saw the Queen start coming down the stairs and I said, "Just a minute, sir." I guess she came back to the castle while I was down in Daddy's workshop.

"Yes," she said in that low voice queens use when they speak to barons.

I went into the hall. I could have stayed there and heard them but I didn't want to. I took a great big breath, tied my shoe, and then I went outside. I thought I would find Sara Dell and we would play something.

It rained and rained, and Baby Julia said God was crying because he had gas. She thought that was the only thing that would make him cry so hard, because Baby Julia had gas all the time from eating too much stuff, and she knew how it felt. There are good rains and bad rains. This rain was the bad kind, because it went on and on and never stopped for days except at night when we went to bed and couldn't go out anyway. It was a very sneaky rain, and gray.

I didn't like it one bit. It wasn't nice in the castle with that rain sneaking down outside, and the Queen and the Princess always yelling at each other, and Daddy gone away. For a while it was exciting to see them yell at each other, and then it wasn't any more. They never said anything new. The best place in the castle was in bed.

Sometimes in the afternoons we would have club meetings in Gregory's garage. Only there wasn't ever much to do, and Baby Julia yelled, and Robert scratched and hopped. Little Arthur let us all feel the kittens moving in the belly of the Russian cat. It felt like there were about a million in there. They slid around under the fur, and it made my stomach hurt to feel them. I thought it would be nice if ladies had babies like cats. Then you could have your whole family all at once and be through.

Gregory got to be a very big guy in the club because his cat Anna was having those kittens. He told Robert that he could watch, and then he got mad at Robert and told him he couldn't watch, either, and

Robert just about cried. Gregory said Eugene and Little Arthur could watch any time. He said that Baby Julia was too little, and that Sara Dell's hair was too long, and that I would make too much noise.

But nobody got to watch after all. Anna went out in the rain and had them at night in the dark.

The next day Gregory's mother's maid found them under a bush. There were six of them. They were little and blind and awful. All they could do was squirm and they didn't even like each other because when they ate they would push each other away. I didn't think they were very nice kittens.

Everybody sat in a circle in the garage to watch them eat. Anna lay over on her side and watched us, while they pulled at the bumps on her stomach. Baby Julia got hungry. She went in and asked Gregory's mother for a sandwich and got a banana one. The rest of the club was very quiet. We watched Anna and Anna watched us, and the kittens made little noises. Two of them weren't getting anything to eat because they got pushed away.

Sara Dell saw it first. "Ooh!" she yelled. "Ooh, ooh, ooh!" That's all she would say for a while. She jumped up and stood by the garage door, pointing at the kittens, yelling ooh as loud as she could. Nobody could make her be quiet until Little Arthur said to shut up.

"What's the matter?" I asked. Her face scared me, it was so red.

"Ooh," said Sara Dell. "Ugh, awful."

Eugene made her say what it was. He said Little Arthur didn't want her to be a vice-president any more unless she told.

"That kitten," said Sara Dell. "Ooooh!"

"Which kitten?" asked Robert.

Everybody got close to look at the kittens but Anna blew breath through her cat teeth and looked mean.

"Yow," yelled Baby Julia. Some banana fell out of her sandwich and got on her shorts. "That kitten's got a hole in its back."

We looked.

Gregory went white and I just about got sick. One of the little ones that wasn't eating any lay on its stomach, and right in the middle of its back was a hole. The fur was all around it, but the hole was red and pink. It was the worst thing I ever saw.

"It's deformed," said Eugene. His eyes were shining behind those glasses. "It's really deformed," he said.

"It is not," yelled Baby Julia. "It's got a big old hole in its back."

"Look at that hole," said Robert. "Just look at that hole."

"Ooh," said Sara Dell. "It's got blood in it."

"I bet that hole goes all the way down to its stomach," said Robert. "I bet if we put milk down it, its stomach would drink the milk."

"You can't put any milk down my kitten's hole,"

said Gregory. He stood up and his hands went back and forth. "You leave that hole alone."

He wouldn't sit back down until Little Arthur told him to.

"Maybe we ought to put a Band-Aid on the hole," I said. "Then when it turns over its blood won't fall out."

"Yeah, but when you took the Band-Aid off the hair would come off too and its skin would hurt," said Sara Dell. "Ooooh."

"I wanna put milk down it," said Baby Julia. "I bet its stomach is real hungry. I bet it would like some milk a whole lot." She had squashed the banana all over her shorts.

"No," Gregory said.

It was getting blacker outside with more rain plopping against the garage door, and before long it would be supper and time to go home. "If we don't do something about that kitten it might up and die," said Sara Dell.

"While it's asleep," said Robert.

We sat in a circle and looked at the box where the kittens were, and at the red hole in that kitten's back.

"How do you reckon it got that hole?" I said.

"Maybe it came with a hole," said Sara Dell.

"Kittens don't come with holes in their backs," yelled Baby Julia. "They come with plain old backs. Like those kittens." She pointed at the rest of them. I thought Anna was a bad mother. She didn't care a thing about the kitten with a hole. She never even looked at it.

"It must have been born that way," said Eugene, very slow. "I never knew that happened."

"I know what it is," said Robert. We looked at him and he made us wait a minute. "It's got a worm down its back," he said. "It's got a worm down there and the worm is eating it up, just like an apple."

"No," said Gregory, "no, no, no, it doesn't have a worm in its back, no, no, no, no." He went on and on, like a song, until Robert punched him. Gregory rocked down and up on his knees and sang "No, no, no," and Robert had to punch him again. Gregory shut up but then he kept bending down and up like a rocking chair. Down and up, down and up.

"Little Arthur thinks you are correct," said Eugene. He put his hands together. "The kitten has a worm in its back and we have to get it out."

"No, no, no," sang Gregory very low. "No worm, no worm." He rocked up and down.

"We've got to get it out," said Sara Dell. "Think about the poor little kitten." You would have thought she was Cherry Ames.

"How would you like to have a worm in your back?" Eugene asked Gregory, and Gregory got whiter than ever.

"Let's pull out the old worm!" yelled Baby Julia.

"No, you can't do that," I said. "It might be way down in its stomach and we might pull out some of its stomach." When I looked at the little kitten, all I could see was the hole. It looked bigger and redder every time, and the kitten looked littler.

"Little Arthur says the club has a duty to kill the worm," said Eugene.

"And make the kitten well," said Sara Dell.

"Little Arthur says this club has a duty to kill the worm and what we have to do is put iodine down the hole," said Eugene. His hands were together tight in front of him. The white of his bones showed through because they were together so tight.

"Yeah," yelled Baby Julia.

"No, no, down the hole," sang Gregory. He was acting very stupid.

Sara Dell went to ask Gregory's mother's maid for some iodine.

"Say you have a cut," said Eugene.

Nobody said anything and we waited. It was getting dark in the garage and Robert turned on the light bulb so we could see the kitten.

Sara Dell came back with the iodine and gave it to Eugene. Eugene turned the top around and around and squeezed the rubber part. The iodine went gurgle and nobody asked to do it but Eugene. He had bright eyes. We all scooted closer and closer to the box and I held my breath. Anna watched us while the other kittens ate. They didn't know that anything at all was going on.

Eugene took the iodine thing and bent down over the box. The little kitten was lying very still, all by itself at the side of the box. Eugene's fingers pushed together and the iodine squirted into the hole. The sides of the hole got redder and shiny wet. Eugene got some more iodine. He did it again and again with very bright eyes. We kept moving closer to the box with small movements. Then Eugene sat back and we waited.

All of a sudden there was a noise from the kitten. It was like a mew and a sigh together. The kitten began to shake all over.

"Ooh, we hurt it," said Sara Dell. We got very close to the box. I didn't want to look but I couldn't stop looking.

The kitten was tiny. It shook, and shook, and pushed its little paws around and around. It made that awful noise again. Like it would be crying if kittens could cry. The hole was red and wet, and the more I looked, the bigger it got. I jerked back and then we were all moving back and away from that box and the kitten. Its paws patted at the blanket in the box with tiny pats. It picked its head up and looked at us for a long time with its blind eyes. Its head fell over onto the blanket and it stopped its shaking.

"I guess it didn't work," said Eugene. He stood up.

"Time to go home," he said, because outside it was dark.

"You killed it," said Sara Dell. "You killed it. I got the iodine and you killed that little kitten." She was crying and she ran out of the garage door.

Robert started to touch it but he didn't. I sat right where I was.

"Poor kitten," said Baby Julia. She giggled and tried to get the banana off her shorts. Baby Julia was too little to know what was going on.

"Dead," said Gregory. He got up slow. "DEAD!" he yelled in a funny high voice. "DEAD!"

"Shut up," said Eugene.

"Do you want your mother to come out here?" said Robert.

"I don't care," said Gregory. He was crying. "I don't care." He started to the door and turned around. "I quit your old club," he said. "I quit right now." Then he went into his house and banged the door.

We stood up. The kitten was tiny lying there, and it was dead but its eyes were still looking at us. I didn't know whether Eugene knew it would die or not when he squirted the iodine. But I knew that Gregory wouldn't tell his mother. That kitten was so little. I almost said I would quit the club too but I didn't, because by then it was too late for me to quit.

The rain came down until I thought it never would stop coming. I remembered all about the Bible and Noah's ark, and I couldn't figure out who I would walk with if we all walked two by two. I thought it would be Daddy and the Queen, but then that would make it me and the Princess; so it must be the Princess and the Queen, and Daddy and me. Only if Tom Cleveland came with us, the Princess would walk with him and then the Queen would walk with Daddy and I didn't know who I would walk with. I thought, maybe I just won't go, but then I remembered about all those nice animals on the ark and thought I would go anyway. I could always walk with a squirrel.

After two days we had a flood. I thought it was a big flood but Daddy said it wasn't. The water in the little creek of the wading house kept coming up, and up, and the water in the river beyond the highway came over the highway. A lot of cars got stuck. Everywhere there were pools of water in the low ground, and Elsie Mae shook her head and said the time was coming sooner than she thought. I said "What time, Elsie Mae?" but she shook her head and made meat loaf, talking real low to herself. The radio man told everybody to put good water in all their pitchers and save it. Daddy didn't go to work. We walked in tall boots beyond the house of Little Arthur to the highway, to stand on the high ground and watch.

The river was brown and bubbly. It looked like cake icing. Pieces of wood and other stuff went by, first ducking under the water and then coming up somewhere else, turning around and around in the brown water. One time a doghouse went by. And a big box sank that said ORANGES in orange letters. After I looked at the water for a long time it felt like I was moving and it was standing still. I was moving the other way. Daddy told me about how bad it was for crops, and how it was all caused by poor land control and things. He said everybody should plant trees.

When we were home again the radio man said that we were declared a disaster area. I got all excited and ran to tell the Princess, but she was playing records and said no, we hadn't either, the disaster area was more to the south. I knew we were in a disaster area anyway, I didn't care what the Princess said. I thought I'd been out in more rain than the Princess. The Victrola played in French, and the Queen was not at home.

That afternoon Sara Dell and Baby Julia and I put on bathing suits and sat in the puddles. When we walked on the grass, water squirted up between our toes, and we pulled at the branches and it rained on us out of the trees. That was a nice afternoon. I went by myself, later and wearing a sweater, to the wading house by the creek.

Water had come up over the rock, and the rock was gone when I poked below the water. It was all gone. The leaves that made the walls of the wading house were brown with mud, and all beat up. I didn't know what had happened to anybody, or where they were. I couldn't find old Grandfather Turtle, or the fishes, or the family of worms. All I could find was mud, and rocks turned over. After a while I thought that everybody was all right, that they were only somewhere else instead of here. The bright lizard had taken them all to a safe place, sliding in front of them like that majorette in the high school. Only I didn't feel good even after I thought that, and very soon I left.

A big Red Cross lady came to the castle with her great white face and a long needle. She said that because we were a disaster area, all the children needed shots. I was nine, too old to cry, but I cried anyway because she was awful.

"Stick out your arm, honey," she said.

"Oh, go on, Susan," said the Queen. "You're a big girl, why don't you act like it for a change?"

"I am not," I told everybody. "I only weigh seventy-eight pounds."

But they made me put my arm out anyway, the Queen holding me around the middle and the Red Cross lady like a big white rock, squeezing my arm tight so

I couldn't move and then hurting me with the needle. The shot wasn't all that bad but I couldn't quit crying. It didn't even hurt but I cried and cried, even after she went away.

The day after the water went down, Frank came back. The sun came out, and the flood was over, and Frank came back like he did every day before the flood. The palace garden was real funny-looking, full of branches and mud, and squashed-down grass and dead flowers. We saw Frank coming from a long way off, but we didn't know when we saw him that it was Frank.

"What's that coming up the road?" asked Elsie Mae, bugging out her eyes.

"Why, I declare I don't know," said the Queen. She went to the window and laughed. I looked too.

"It's FRANK!" I yelled. I could tell by the gray legs under all the stuff. I laughed and laughed. You couldn't see any head at all, or any bit of Frank above the waist. Only those gray legs, pointing together a little bit at the knees. From the middle up he was all clothes, and food, and big brown paper boxes with red X's on them. Everything jiggled and squirmed as he came, but nothing fell off. When he got close enough, the Queen opened the door and said, "My goodness, Frank, this flood must have really wiped you out." She had worry in her voice.

Frank didn't say anything back. He started putting

all the things one by one on the wet, squishy yard. He put the brown boxes down first, and food boxes on top of them, and clothes on top of them. When he had taken off enough things so that we could see his face, his face was grinning. He grinned and grinned. We stood behind the screen door in a row and watched him grin.

"Frank," said the Queen again. "Frank, please tell me. Maybe we can help you." Her long fingers with red tips went tap, tap, on the edge of the screen door. She leaned forward and then back when she couldn't see for the sun. "This flood must have really destroyed everything you own, didn't it? Well, didn't it? I mean, it must have, if you were forced to get all these things from the Red Cross."

Frank grinned. He squished his feet in the mud. "Har," he said.

"Oh, don't be embarrassed," said the Queen. "How badly did this flood hurt you, Frank?"

"Flood never titched me," said Frank. "Har, har."

"Well," said the Queen. "Well, really," she said. "I never in all my life." She went away from the door upstairs, and mad. When Queens are mad, you leave them alone. I didn't know quite why the Queen was mad, though, or why Elsie Mae was laughing.

I went over to Sara Dell's. She came back with me to look at all Frank's things. They were piled on top of each other, and they made a small crazy house in our wet yard. We walked around it three time to look.

"Where'd he get all that stuff?" said Sara Dell.

I said I didn't know, maybe from the Red Cross, but that it made my mother mad and made Elsie Mae laugh.

"Huh," said Sara Dell.

The sun came shining back from all the pools of water, and in every yard somebody was cleaning up.

"What do you want to do?" I said to Sara Dell. "I don't care."

"Mama said some new kids are moving in that house up the road," said Sara Dell. "We could go look at them."

"O.K.," I said, because I never had looked at new kids before. All the kids I knew were old kids, except at school. I thought it would be a good day to do a new thing since the sun was out and the flood was over. We walked across the yard in boots, up the road to the house where the Perkinses used to live. A big truck was outside.

"See?" said Sara Dell. We stood behind a bush. "See?" she said.

"I don't see anything," I said, "except that old truck."

Then the door of the Perkins' house opened and some men wearing blue clothes came out. They began to take the tables and chairs and things out of the truck. A lady stood in the door and watched.

Sara Dell sat down in a wet place under the bush

"I'm Nancy Drew," she said. "You can be my chum George or my chum Bess. Either one you want."

"I want to be Nancy Drew," I said.

"I said it first," Sara Dell said, and she was right, so I said I would be Nancy's chum Bess. I told Nancy to be quiet, since we were spies.

In a little while, two kids came out. They walked around their yard and looked at the things in it, and the girl said did Henry think Daddy would put up a swing. They looked like nice kids, and they both had short hair. Henry's was yellow and the girl's was red and fuzzy. Henry was a little bit fat.

"Maybe they want to be in the club," I said.

"I don't know if Little Arthur would like them," said Nancy Drew. "They are awful new."

"We can ask him," I said.

Nancy Drew and I spied on those kids until their mother said for them to come in. Then we left, walking through water so dogs couldn't track us by our smell, and running across open yards so no enemies could spot us.

That night the Princess explained to me about Frank while she was brushing her hair. She said that Frank had gotten his whole crazy house from the government, that he had cheated the government to get all those things. Food and clothes were free if your house was washed away, she said. But Frank's house wasn't washed away and he got them anyway. The Princess said that

Democrats were stupid and that the New Deal was stupid because people like Frank would always be around to take unfair advantage of things. The Princess said she had a good mind to write somebody a letter about it.

She said Frank would only work so long every day because if he worked too long he wouldn't get any relief.

"What's relief?" I said. The long hair of the Princess was alive. Every time she brushed it, it would jump and jerk all by itself.

"Why don't you get ready for bed," she said.

That day was a good day. It should have been a good day, because it was the day of the end of the flood and the start of summer again, and it was a fine day. We saw the new kids, Henry and the girl with the fuzzy hair, and Frank cheated the government. I knew that the government was big and important. I knew it was scary, and red, white and blue, and that everybody did what it said no matter what. You had to. It grabbed Daddy's money and put men in its army, and it was a big thing. A bigger thing than anything else I knew of except God. But Frank cheated it. Old Frank, who was gray all over and said "har" and worked in the yard, he had fixed the Lord and then cheated the government. I thought he was really brave. He got his crazy house free from the government, and then he cleaned up our yard. It was a nice day.

Only after that the days were not so fine any more, and things started to go very fast, and my summer head came back. Daddy was away for two days. While he was gone the Baron came to the castle a lot, and one day he brought me a little box of candy. The next day he brought the Princess some stuff to smell good with, but the Princess didn't like it. She was ugly about it. The day after that the Princess went away to the lake with Tom Cleveland and she didn't tell anybody good-bye.

Nothing was nice even though the sun was out. Sara Dell and I went to the drugstore for ice-cream cones and on a rack of magazines in the drugstore there was a bad magazine with a girl on the front. The main story in it was, "I Sold My Body for a Bride Doll," that some twelve-year-old kid wrote. We didn't read the story. Sara Dell said it might be nasty. We looked at the front of the magazine, and licked our ice cream, and patted the drugstore man's dog on the head, and Sara Dell's mother took us home when she was through at the beauty shop. Robert came over to the castle after lunch, and said Little Arthur had taught him to conjugate verbs. Robert said:

"I will get mine.
You will get yours.
He, she, it will get his.
We will get ours.
They will get theirs.
Everybody will get it."

I told Robert to go home, and he said there was a club meeting that night at the clubhouse. "You will get yours," he said. "He, she, it will get his," he said. Then he went home.

I started to go down to the wading house, but when I thought about it I decided not to go there any more for a while. Because everybody wouldn't be there, they would be far away in that safe place where they had gone with the bright lizard leading and it would be lonely in the wading house.

Daddy was at the castle for dinner. He came in and put down his bag in the hall just before Elsie Mae had it ready.

"Where's your mother?" he said.

"Upstairs," I told him, and he went right up there. I went in the kitchen with a *Terry and the Pirates* comic book and while Elsie Mae and I waited for them to come down I read it.

Dinner was no fun. Nobody talked but me. The Queen was like the Snow Queen in that story in the blue book. Her face was white like ice. Daddy looked awful. I asked him if he had flu, or if he was sick or what, and he said, "In a way." Daddy smiled at me, a slow smile that hurt his face a little, and then the Queen began talking fast about what the flood had done to the rosebushes. Her hands went back and forth like birds, and everything was good again.

Elsie Mae was in the kitchen when I went out the door. Her feet were blue-shiny, and her white sleeves were pulled up high so she could wash a big pan. I saw something then that I never saw before. On the top part of Elsie Mae's black arm was a big blue heart with a ruffle.

"Elsie Mae," I yelled so loud she dropped the pan and splashed water onto the floor. "Elsie Mae, where did you get that blue heart on your arm? That heart up on your arm with a ruffle?"

Elsie Mae said, "Hee, hee, hee," and looked out the window.

I got closer so I could look at it better. "Can I feel it?" I said.

"I reckon," said Elsie Mae. "Ain't nothing but a tattoo, hee, hee."

I felt it with a finger, and it felt like the whole rest of Elsie Mae's arm. "How'd you get it on there?" I said. "Can you wash it off?"

"No, honey," said Elsie Mae. "I reckon it's on there for good. I reckon I'm branded sure enough."

"When did you get it on there," I said.

"It was a real long time ago," Elsie Mae said. She was washing the pan again and looking out the window where dark was starting to come. "I was mighty young, and we were all out at this traveling show, riding the rides, and eating stuff, and my boy friend and me we got these tattoos."

I stood on one foot and told her I thought that was pretty stupid. Now she couldn't wash it off. "I still don't see how come you did it," I said.

"I was pretty silly that night," said Elsie Mae. "Hee, hee, hee. I sure was silly that time, hee."

I thought she was too. Elsie Mae's feet twinkled and she kept on laughing while she washed the pan, and I went to the club meeting.

It was dark in the clubhouse, and it smelled like old rain. Robert conjugated for everybody until Little Arthur told him to shut up. Gregory wasn't there, and nobody had thought he would be there, and that made us more of a club. Eugene's eyes looked at us one by one. "Little Arthur says this is the night of the test," he said.

"Goody," yelled Baby Julia. "If there's anything I like it's a good old test."

"You never had a test in your whole life," Robert said to Baby Julia. "Shut up."

"Little Arthur says that Gregory was unfaithful to the club," Eugene told us. "And now no one else must ever be unfaithful to the club again. Little Arthur is sure that Robert will not be unfaithful," he said, and we looked at Robert. Robert grinned. He had lost a tooth since that morning. "Little Arthur is sure of Robert, but he is not sure of Susan and Sara Dell and Baby Julia."

"Why not?" asked Sara Dell, in the voice she always used when you hurt her feelings. "Why isn't Little Arthur sure of me?"

"You have to deserve it," said Eugene. "Little Arthur wants you to prove it."

"I wanna prove it," yelled Baby Julia. "You tell me what and I'll do it right now. You just tell me what."

Eugene took a Boy Scout flashlight out of his pocket. "Little Arthur wants," said Eugene, talking very slowly then, "Little Arthur wants Susan and Baby Julia and Sara Dell to take off their pants and walk in front of the rest of the club." Robert drew his breath in very much and sat up straight, and I felt funny in my stomach and my legs.

"That's nasty," said Sara Dell. "I won't do it. I'm going home, goodbye." But she stayed in the clubhouse sitting on the ground, and never moved at all.

"All right, Sara Dell," said Eugene. "If that's the way you feel about it. This is a test. This is what Little Arthur says. If you don't want to be in the club, you don't have to be in the club." Eugene took off his glasses and cleaned them on his shirt, and without the glasses the eyes were even more awful than before.

"O.K.," said Baby Julia. She jumped up and took off

her shorts and white panties with lace and Eugene turned the Boy Scout flashlight on her while she walked around the clubhouse. Baby Julia was so fat she jiggled, and she was bright pink and then brown where her bathing suit had not been. She laughed and jiggled up and down around the clubhouse. It was pretty funny, I guess. Sara Dell went next, with her mouth all screwed up together. Her panties had flowers on them, and I felt awful because mine didn't have any flowers or any lace or anything. They were plain old white ones. When I walked around I didn't look at anybody. I put my head back and looked at the top of the clubhouse, and I almost fell down on Robert because I couldn't see where I was going.

Then the club meeting was over, and Little Arthur was pleased, and we put back on our panties and our shorts and ran down that path through the bushes to home. Away up in the mountain a dog barked as we came out of the bushes into the yard.

I went to bed right after the club meeting but then I woke up suddenly and the moon was all over my bed. Outside was like morning, only it was white instead of yellow. The moon had come down from the sky to sit on a tree in the field behind the dogbushes, and the man in it was laughing and laughing. I thought I would get up and go out in all that white. I didn't know why I woke up, because most of the time when you wake up like that in the middle of the night you have to go to the bathroom, and I didn't even have to go. I didn't have to do anything. I felt sort of funny but I knew I wasn't sick, and I put on my pink rabbit-fur shoes and a shirt over my pajamas. I looked one time out the window. All the white light was out there and it looked real pretty.

The house was dark inside, away from the windows, and you could tell everybody in it was asleep. I didn't turn on any lights. I went down the stairs, through the dining room and through the kitchen, and out the kitchen door. I didn't stop one time. I didn't even think about what I would do when I got outside.

It was bright, with a white light coming up from the ground. I walked and walked, out of the yard under the dogbushes and into the field. I was the only thing in the night besides the moon. I sat down in the middle of the field and crossed my feet.

It was a long time before I saw them coming. They came one by one in a line, out of the trees where the mountains started to go up. They didn't bark. They walked one by one, slowly, across the field to me. I thought of what Elsie Mae had told me, about dogs and dog packs and how they came down from the mountains in winter looking for food and would eat anything they found, but I wasn't scared.

I sat there and watched them.

They came very close. The one in front was the biggest dog I ever saw. He was all white, so that you could hardly tell him from the moonlight. He held his head up high, and picked up his feet when he walked. His hair was thick and there was a lot of it, and I thought he looked like a king. The other dogs came behind him in a line. They were all different sizes and darker colors. None of them barked. They walked in a circle around me, looking at me, thirteen of them. I sat there and watched them, and after they walked one time in the circle around me they started away across that white field. I looked at them until they were past the trees and into the mountain, walking in a line and stepping high, and I couldn't see them any longer. Then I got up and walked back across the field and into the castle.

I took off my pink rabbit shoes and got into bed. The minute I got in bed I started turning over and over, until I was all tied up in the sheets on the bed. I was real scared for a little while. I thought I would like to say my prayers again so I lay there and tried to, but I couldn't remember how they went. It was the first time I couldn't remember and it scared me. I couldn't pray to the God of the thunder, or the skinny Jesus walking on the waters, or even to the little pink Baby Jesus. I couldn't remember how. I thought about the moonlight, the white everywhere, and about Little Arthur because I knew that he had been out in that moonlight somewhere too, and I thought about the dogs. That king dog was beautiful.

What if the dogs had eaten me up, I thought. I don't know why they didn't do it. I thought about how it would be to be eaten up. I wouldn't be me any more, I would be little pieces of me inside the dogs. I got an awful feeling in my stomach, and my head was very light. I got scared. I knew I had to say my prayers but I still couldn't remember them. The whole night outside my window was white, and I was all tied up in my sheet.

I didn't think I ever went to sleep but then I woke up all of a sudden again and this time it was morning and Elsie Mae was right there giggling. I didn't know any more whether I had been outside or what.

"Hee, hee, hee," said Elsie Mae. "You sure knows how to tear up a bed. I guess you had you some dream."

The next day I talked to the new kids. They came with their dog, walking down the road, and I was sitting out on the front porch with Elsie Mae. It was a nice day.

"Hi," they said.

"You say hi," said Elsie Mae to me.

"Hi," I said.

"Where do you all go swimming around here?" the girl asked.

"We don't go swimming," I said. "We hate it."

"Oh," said the boy, and they walked on down the road with their dog. Elsie Mae put her knitting down on the porch.

"Susan Tobey," she said, "that was right ugly. That was the ugliest thing I ever saw you do."

I got up and went in the castle. I knew it was ugly. I liked those new kids just about more than I ever liked anybody, I liked them so much that it made my head hurt. I wasn't ever so ugly before, and it was awful.

That afternoon Sara Dell came to the castle with her mother. Sara Dell's mother was little and fat, and when she smiled big crinkles went all over her face. I thought she would be a nice mother to sit in the lap of, like Sara Dell used to do sometimes, but then Sara Dell's mother was not a Queen. She was not even a member of the Court. Sara Dell's mother had a pie with a pink napkin on it, and I thought it was very nice of her to bring us the pie but I didn't see why she did it. I was afraid Elsie Mae would get mad.

"Sara Dell thought you might like to go visiting with

us, Susan," said Sara Dell's mother. "Mr. Tate is very sick and so we're going to take Mrs. Tate a pie."

I looked at Sara Dell and she made a face.

I stepped on one foot with my other foot. "I don't know," I said. "I'd really like to go but I have a lot of things I have to do."

Sara Dell's mother laughed until the crinkles went everywhere on her face. "Come on," she said, and we walked along the road together, up the driveway and the long high walk to the Tates' house.

"I don't want to go, Mama," said Sara Dell. "I want to go home. Old Mrs. Tate's a witch."

"Why, Sara Dell," said her mother, "I don't know where you pick up ideas like that. Mrs. Tate is not a witch. That's a terrible thing to say. She's a sweet nice old lady, and I'm sure she's very lonely. Oh, look at those roses," said Sara Dell's mother. She leaned over and touched a yellow one with her hand. They were nice roses, all colors and kinds along the walk and stretched out on either side of it until a rock wall stopped them. I thought how much fun I could have if I was a bee.

"Let's don't go and say we did," Sara Dell said when her mother rang the doorbell. The front door to the Tates' house was big and dark and heavy, and it looked like it might be about a million years old. We could hear Mrs. Tate coming on slow feet for a long time before she got there, and the door sounded like it hurt when she opened it. Mrs. Tate was much smaller than I had thought. She was very tiny, and white, and her hands shook so much that she had to put them together to make them stop.

When Sara Dell's mother gave her the pie she said, "My, wasn't that a nice thing to do?," and Sara Dell's mother said, "That's what neighbors are for," and Sara Dell said, "What?," and then Mrs. Tate said, "Oh, what lovely children," and we all smiled.

The house smelled like real old dirt, or dead things. It was quiet in the living room where we sat. All the chairs were big and green, and the sunlight coming in at the window was full of twirling dust. There was a corsage under a glass bell on a little round table. The flowers looked like new, and the ribbons and the pearl-headed pin, but I knew they were old. They were ages and ages old. Maybe Mrs. Tate had worn them at a dance when she was young. I looked at Mrs. Tate and then I thought she was never young. The flowers were still as a statue under the clear glass bell.

I felt like I had been sitting on that chair for about a million years, and that I might sit there for a million years more with the green walls and the twirling dust around me, and the funny thing was that I didn't think I would mind. Then someone made a noise away in the back of the house. It was not a noise like a person would make, but like a dog, and Mrs. Tate said, "Oh, he must want something. I'm afraid you'll have to excuse me for a second, since the nurse is out." When she stood up she looked like she wasn't really there. She was so little, and white, and so old that she wasn't Mrs. Tate any more. She was only something old and white that I didn't know anything about.

"Oh, we have to be leaving," said Sara Dell's mother. "If you ever need anything whatsoever just call us, and Clarence or I will be right up. Any time of the day or night."

Sara Dell whispered and said that Mr. Tate had T.B. and that he lived in an iron lung, and then she told me what an iron lung was.

When we were out of the house and back on the walk, the sun was a lot brighter and the air was better than it was before, and Sara Dell and I kicked two rocks in front of us and skipped all the way down the hill.

Everybody was there already, on the grass under the big tree in Robert's front yard. Baby Julia was eating a pink rose, and one petal was stuck to her neck.

I almost hadn't gone to the club meeting. I had been

busy with eating a banana and listening to the radio and bending my feet, all at the same time, but then the Baron and the Queen came downstairs and when they made me turn off the radio and told me why didn't I go wash my feet, I thought about the club meeting and left.

Robert was picking scabs and when I looked under Sara Dell's arm, sure enough she was sweating. A wet place like a dark new moon. Sara Dell had grown up a lot that summer.

"The time is here," Eugene was saying, and I thought about how white he stayed, how he never got brown in the sun like we did. "Little Arthur says this cannot go on. He says that some of our members are working against us in this club, and Little Arthur has made a plan to stop it. If you don't do the plan then you're out of the club and something bad will happen to you quick."

"What?" asked Robert.

"Little Arthur knows," said Eugene. He smiled. "To-morrow night we meet here at ten o'clock. I don't care how you get here but you'd better get here. Then we're going to fix old Mrs. Tate. That's the first thing Little Arthur wants us to do."

"She's nice," Sara Dell said. "We went to see her today with Mama and she's nice. We took her a pie." She is nice, I thought. But she smells old.

Robert caught a fly and let it go.

"All right, Sara Dell," said Eugene quietly. He smiled again. Sara Dell said she would come at ten o'clock, for him not to worry about her, that she would be there early.

"Little Arthur says are there any other questions," Eugene said.

"Yeah," yelled Baby Julia. "I wanna put the new kids in the club."

"Little Arthur hates the new kids," Eugene said. His eyes were flat and white. "Little Arthur knows something very bad that will happen to them."

"Can we do it?" yelled Baby Julia.

"Yes," said Eugene. And then he told us what it was. It was awful. We all nodded and smiled at Little Arthur, and I got my funny summer head back. It was fat, too full of things. My head never used to be that full, not at the beginning of everything. I could remember the day that summer started and how nice it was.

"Ten o'clock tomorrow night," said Eugene.

"When can we do it to the new kids?" Sara Dell asked.

It was almost suppertime.

"That comes after," Eugene told us.

"Goody, goody, goody," yelled Baby Julia. She rolled over and over in the green grass and we all got up and went home while Baby Julia was still rolling.

Frank was working in the yard, bending over the flowers by the castle wall like he was part of the wall.

"I'm here," I yelled when I went into the castle. I don't know why I yelled that because most of the time I never yelled it, I just went into the castle. It was funny in there and I knew something was wrong but I didn't know what it was that was different. "Elsie Mae," I yelled, then I thought about how Elsie Mae was off that day because somebody she knew was getting married. "Betty," I yelled, for the Princess, but then I remembered that the Princess was away at the lake with Tom Cleveland. It was time for Daddy to be home but Daddy wasn't at home either. I looked all over downstairs, and yelled down in the basement, and no one was anywhere. Outside it was getting dark so I turned on one light in the living room and got a magazine to look at. I saw all these pictures some man took in the snow, all about seals and snow animals, and some more pictures where doctors were cutting up a man on a table. The table had a big bright light over it so that the doctors could see what they were doing and wouldn't miss.

Then all of a sudden I stood up and walked up the

stairs and into the chambers of the Queen, and everything there was wrong. I put on a light and it was worse. All the shimmery dresses were gone from the closets, and the bottles and jewels were gone from the dresser, and small things, like stockings, were thrown and fallen all over the room. Then I knew what was the matter and what had been the matter all afternoon, and I sat down on the floor and picked up one of the stockings and there was a run in it. The funny thing was that I was not surprised. I sat on the floor while it got darker and darker outside, until it got very dark, with the stocking in my hand until Daddy and Betty came home.

I went down the stairs with the stocking and said hi to them, and Daddy kissed the top part of my head and Betty was blowing her nose. She cooked hot dogs but she kept burning them and saying things like damn when she did it. Betty never looked at Daddy and Daddy never looked at anybody. I looked at everybody all the time. The hot dogs were awful and nobody ate very much.

" 'Just singin' in the rain,' " the radio sang.

"Turn it off," said Daddy.

I turned the little knob and we got the *Town Crier*. "Young tragedy. Jimmy Davidson of Baltimore, Maryland, has a new idea about how to win girls and influence their parents," it said. "Jimmy put up a giant sign in a vacant lot across from his girl's home which said, 'Pattie, I love you. Will you marry me?,' but unfortunately he misspelled Pattie. Jimmy Davidson says he is still in love but may have to resort to a more conventional approach due to Pattie's unfortunate reaction."

Betty began to laugh. Her hair fell into her face and she laughed and laughed until she was almost crying. I couldn't eat my hot dog. It was too red. I took it out of its bread and rolled it around on the table and it was too red all over. It was the reddest thing I ever saw. "Look," I said to them, but Daddy was putting something in a glass for Betty to drink and then they were taking my hands and we were going into the living room.

"What are you going to do about it?" Betty said. "That's the main thing. I mean, what the hell are we supposed to do now? I can't even walk down the street now, I'm so embarrassed. And it's your fault. It's all your fault. You just sat around. Nothing had to happen like this. You're really weak, you know? A very weak man."

Daddy said, "Betty, believe me, there wasn't a thing I could do. Nothing in the world. Frankly, I was surprised that she stayed this long. I'm sorry. Please believe that I'm very sorry for you and for Susan." Daddy's voice sounded like mine did the time I had a cold and couldn't go out in the last snow of the winter.

"Look," said Betty. "I guess it took me a while to catch on, but I did. I know all about her. But you didn't have to let this happen." Betty swished the ice around and around in her glass. I was getting sleepy and my eyes kept falling together even when I put my fingers up for props. The fingers kept falling off like they weren't even hooked on to my hand.

Daddy was walking up and down the room talking very fast to Betty, putting his hands on his hair and putting them out in the air. I didn't listen much because I was thinking about birds and when I closed my eyes I could see them, blue ones, high in lots of tall trees. Once I opened my eyes and Daddy was still walking and telling things to Betty, and Betty sat still with her legs crossed and her mouth all bent up in an ugly way. She was not so pretty then. Daddy talked about how he met the Queen when he was an artist, and then how he quit being an artist to make some money. He said he didn't ever have any choices but he didn't want any either. He said couldn't Betty understand anything that simple?

"You know what I think?" said Betty in a voice like a rock. "I think this is all really trite and I'm going over to the Clevelands' now. They asked me this afternoon."

"Betty," Daddy said. Betty pushed out her cigarette in the ash tray and went upstairs, and after a while she came down with a bag.

"I'm sorry that you feel this way," Daddy said politely. "You're still my daughter, you know. I love you."

"Sure," said Betty. She left. Outside then I could

hear the car going and the little rocks squnching in the driveway when the car went over them and away.

"Come on, Susan," said Daddy. "We'll talk about this some more tomorrow." Then he kissed me and closed the door and went away, but I remembered the night the Queen came, when she kissed me smelling like all those flowers. It was quiet in the house and I was almost asleep when my window went bang. It went bang, crack, at me, and when I went over to look out there was Little Arthur and the whole club in my back yard.

I got up and put on my shorts and a yellow tee shirt and went out through the kitchen, not trying to be quiet because I was pretty sure that Daddy had gone out. I could tell by the way the house felt. I got my green sweater from the closet in the hall because the nights were getting cooler then.

"Little Arthur says hurry," Eugene said. "Tonight we do the biggest thing yet."

"Oh goody," yelled Baby Julia.

I couldn't see anybody, only feel them around me in the dark because the moon was behind lots of clouds. The wind blew too, and up on the hill the Tates' house was black.

"I feel like it's looking at me," I said.

"What's looking at you?" asked Robert. We were going fast and low up the path through the bushes.

"That house," I said, and my legs got too little to take me along.

"Little Arthur thinks Susan is acting like a silly, stupid girl," said Eugene.

"No I'm not either." I got mad then. "You know I'm not a scaredy-cat. I wouldn't be here if I was a scaredy-cat."

We went into the clubhouse for just one minute. "We're going to fix Mrs. Tate good," said Eugene.

"Why?" asked Robert. I couldn't see anybody at all in the dark.

"Because Little Arthur hates her and he wants to." I wanted it too. I could close my eyes and see Mrs. Tate and her long clothes and the little folds in the old white skin on her face. I hated her.

"What are we going to do to her?" asked Sara Dell. She was breathing hard.

"Little Arthur wants you to think of it," Eugene said. "Little Arthur already knows. He wants you to think of it now. What does old Mrs. Tate like more than anything else?"

"Her flowers," yelled Baby Julia. "I know that. I'm the nurse."

"So what are we going to do to them?" Eugene asked in a very soft voice.

"Tear them up." I knew.

"Tear up all her stupid roses. They're the things she likes the best. Those dumb roses." I laughed and laughed. It was the best idea I ever had.

"Right," said Eugene. "Little Arthur says we'd better get started right now." We all stood up and then Eugene stopped for a minute. He said, "And Little Arthur has a special surprise for us after we tear up the roses. It's a game. Little Arthur says that you can't say a word until we get up to the rose garden and he tells you how to play the game."

Sara Dell had a cold and she was sneezing and making frog noises all the way through the meeting.

"I want to go get a handkerchief," she said.

I thought she was dumb to say it, because I knew that Little Arthur would never let her go, but he surprised me and told her to go ahead. "We'll wait for you up here. The later we go the better it is," Eugene said.

I went with Sara Dell because she pulled at my hand so I knew she was scared to go by herself. We ran through all the bushes, fast down the path and holding hands all the way, and I waited in the dark beside the porch of Sara Dell's house while she went in to get the handkerchief. The light was shining out of the windows and the porch door but it didn't quite hit me. Inside the house I could see Sara Dell's mama and her daddy playing cards and they looked real happy.

Sara Dell came out with the handkerchief and she had to give it to me on account of I was crying. This made Sara Dell mad. She went back in and got another handkerchief, a yellow one, and when she came back out again I had quit. We took a short cut through the back yard of the palace, both of us running so that Little Arthur wouldn't be mad at us.

When we got back to the clubhouse they were ready, and no one said a word. Little Arthur went in front and Robert in back, with everybody else in the middle. We ran through all the fruit trees and things and went over the little stone wall to where the roses were. I had to help Baby Julia get over the wall. Everybody started digging in the soft cool dirt with their hands around the bottoms of the bushes. Then we pulled them up and threw them on the ground and laughed, and I could feel the house on the hill look at me and I laughed harder. We pulled them up and pulled them up, until Eugene said, "All right. Little Arthur says for you to stop now."

We stopped where we were and my stomach felt funny and sick when my laughing had ended.

Baby Julia didn't want to quit. She kept pulling up the bushes and sometimes eating the petals, and giggling. Her face was black from dirt.

"Little Arthur says for Baby Julia to quit."

"O.K.," she yelled, and sat down plop in the dirt. "What are we gonna do NOW?" she yelled.

"We are going to play a new game," said Eugene. "This is a game that nobody but Little Arthur has ever played."

"Oh goody," yelled Baby Julia, jumping up and down.

"Shut up," Eugene told her. When we were all quiet again he said, "The name of this game is Iron Lung."

"That's what you have in hospitals when you're sick," Sara Dell said. "That's what Mama says Mr. Tate has now." When she said "Mr. Tate" everybody looked up at the house but we couldn't really see it. All we could see was a black hump stuck onto the sky.

"Anyway, this is the way you play Iron Lung," Eugene said, and all of us looked at him again. "It's sort of like Nurse and Doctor. It's a variation."

"What's a variation?" yelled Baby Julia.

"It's a new way to play," I told her. I could spell it too. I guess I knew more words than anybody else in the club, but it hadn't ever done me any good.

"Like Nurse and Doctor?" asked Sara Dell. She liked to play Nurse and Doctor. She was always the nurse.

"I'm the nurse," yelled Baby Julia, and everybody told her to shut up so hard that we scared her.

"No, Sara Dell is the nurse this time," said Eugene. "Robert is the doctor. Susan is sick, and Little Arthur and I are the Iron Lung."

"Me," said Baby Julia in her crying voice. "What's me?"

"You can be the hospital," Eugene said. "Little Arthur

wants you to be the hospital. It's the biggest thing of all," he said to make her happy. "O.K., start. Little Arthur and I will go right over here until the doctor is ready for us." He and Little Arthur went behind a big bush.

We started with me coming into the doctor's office. "I'm sick," I said. "Can you help me?"

Sara Dell the nurse felt my wrist to see if my heart was still going, and all of a sudden we were not Sara Dell and Robert and Baby Julia and me: all of a sudden we were real. Maybe it was because we couldn't see each other very well in the dark, but we weren't any longer who we were. I couldn't breathe. I couldn't talk either. My throat got all tiny and hurting, and I could barely tell the nurse what was wrong with me. "I've been sick for three days," I said. "I've been too sick to come to the doctor." I couldn't stand up any more; I was very weak.

"Here, lie down," the nurse said. She was clean and white, and she helped me lie down in the dirt. I got flat on my back on the ground and my stomach was going hard up and down and I tried to breathe with my mouth open but it didn't help and I still couldn't breathe. The nurse felt my wrist again.

"Pulse is very rapid, doctor," she said.

"Let's see," said the doctor. "Hmmmmm. We've already tried penicillin. Hmmm."

"Oh, she's really sick," said the nurse. "I'm scared."

"We'll try the oxygen tent," said the doctor.

The nurse and the doctor put something over my head so that the black all around me became thick and crashing in on my head and I knew I was dying. I moved my arms and my legs, trying to get out of the oxygen tent, but the doctor and the nurse held me there on my back in the dirt.

"She's going out of her mind now," said the doctor. "It's the fever."

Then I couldn't breathe at all and I was too tired to move. I felt like I was floating on the water. The oxygen made my head light.

"The oxygen doesn't seem to be working, doctor," said the nurse.

I was dark and dying.

"I guess we'll have to bring in the Iron Lung," the doctor said.

I tried to yell and say no but I couldn't talk and I couldn't breathe either because I was so sick, and they held my hands and my legs down hard. They took away the oxygen tent and then I could see sky, but I couldn't breathe at all without the oxygen.

"Relax," said the nurse. "We're trying to help you."

"Iron Lung, please," the doctor said, and snapped his fingers.

Then all of a sudden Little Arthur and Eugene came running out of nowhere and they were the Iron Lung.

They jumped on me and pulled down my shorts and they were going up and down, up and down, up and down, on me with no clothes on, and they were the Iron Lung, and the doctor said, "One, two, one, two." The nurse said, "I think you're going too fast." I was going down and down into the earth, and the Iron Lung was hurting me between my legs, and the dirt was coming up from all around to cover me, cool and friendly, coming up to cover me because I was dying.

"What are you all doing anyway?" a clear voice said, high and loud. The Iron Lung jumped off me and I could see again, but I couldn't get up from the ground. My legs wouldn't work. The moon was out, and because I had been blind and sick for so long, I could see him like he was standing in the sunlight. Old Gregory was on top of the wall, and the moon was very bright on him and on us. I could see every inch of Gregory standing skinny and straight on that wall. "What are you doing?" he asked. "Why doesn't Susan have any shorts on?" He asked them, not me, but nobody told him and I couldn't move or talk. I looked at my legs and they weren't tan any more; they looked like white rock in the moonlight.

Gregory looked at all of us. "What's going on?" he asked again.

"Nothing, stupid," said Eugene, pulling at a rosebush. "Little Arthur says for you to go away. He hates you."

"Well, I hate him," Gregory said, walking up and down on the wall like an army general. Sara Dell sucked her breath in sharp. "I don't have to do anything Little Arthur says. He can't tell me what to do," Gregory said. He looked tall up there on the wall, and I thought maybe he had grown that summer.

I got up from the dirt and put on my panties and my shorts. I was hurting from the Iron Lung and I felt awful.

"I think you're wrong, Gregory," said Eugene. He said it very low, so that you almost couldn't hear him, but it made you hear him more than ever. "I don't think you mean that, Gregory. I don't think you've considered what you're saying. Little Arthur says you're an ass, Gregory," Eugene said with a flat face.

"I'm sorry," yelled Gregory in a high voice like Sara Dell giggling. "I'm sorry, I'm sorry, I'm sorry." He said it like a song, the way he had done about the kittens, and he rocked up and down and back and forth with his feet together on the wall. Then he jumped off the wall and landed on the other side, and because we were all quiet we could hear his feet running away through the bushes. They stopped for a second and he yelled, "I'm gonna tell," in a big voice, and then ran on.

Robert started to go over the wall and after Gregory, but by the time he started it was already too late so he stopped before he even got to the wall. We were all stopped, like when you play that game Statue. Somebody swings you around and around and when they let you go, you have to stay just the way you are until the swinger says "unfreeze." That is the way we were in the rosebushes. We were all white and still, we were all just swung and frozen, and I was hurting from the Iron Lung.

"Let's go," said Sara Dell after a minute. "I'm scared."

"What are we gonna do now?" yelled Baby Julia, pulling up a bush. It was just about the only one left. "I wanna play some more Iron Lung. I'm the hospital."

"Little Arthur says it's time to go," said Eugene, and we climbed back over the wall and went up the path in a row. It was Little Arthur and Eugene, then Baby Julia and Sara Dell and me, and Robert in the back. Nobody said a word.

When we got to Robert's house, his mother was standing black against the yellow living-room light in the door, like a paper doll. She said that Robert's father wanted to see us all inside immediately. Going inside was like coming out of a movie; everybody blinked and blinked. Sara Dell was crying. Her mother was there too, sitting on a sofa, and Sara Dell went over and sat on her mother. I sat on Sara Dell's mother's lap too. It must have almost killed her because we were so big.

Robert's father came out of the room where he read his books and sat down where we were. His glasses were even thicker than Gregory's. Gregory wasn't there, but then I didn't think he would be. I looked around. Sara Dell's hair was all tangled. She was crying and her mother was patting us both like puppies. Robert stood up tall with his hands behind his back and looked at the ceiling. We were all dirty.

"I'm hungry," yelled Baby Julia. "I wanna go home."

Robert's mother gave her a Hershey bar. "I wanna nother one," she said, and she got that too.

Robert's father had tired eyes from reading so many books. He did something like that for a living.

"Gregory's mother just called and told us what you've been doing tonight," he said. "It was a very cruel and destructive thing to do."

"What was?" asked Robert, playing very dumb. He kept looking at the ceiling like something exciting was going on up there.

"You know," said Robert's father. "Uprooting Mrs. Tate's roses."

"What roses?" I asked, but I had dirt all over my tee shirt. Robert's father looked at me and I felt awful.

"Don't lie to me," he said. "You tore up the flowers.

The important thing is, why? Why did you tear them up?"

Little Arthur told us to, I thought, but then I remembered that I was the one who had thought of tearing them up. I couldn't remember why we had done it.

Nobody said anything at all and then Baby Julia sat up straight with Hershey bar all over her chin. "Because Little Arthur said to. He taught us how to play Iron Lung too," she said.

"Wait a minute," said Sara Dell's mother from where she was under Sara Dell and me. "Who's little Arthur?"

"Yes," said Robert's father. "Who is Arthur?"

"There isn't any child named Arthur in the neighborhood," said Robert's mother. "I knew someone else must have been influencing them. Usually they're so good."

"Just a minute, Mary," said Robert's father. He looked at all of us again, one by one.

"Now who's little Arthur?" he said.

"He has a cape and big black boots and a gun," I said. "And he's older than you are, sir."

"A gun!" said Sara Dell's mother.

"And a big HAT!" yelled Baby Julia. "He showed us lots of stuff."

"I didn't want to," Sara Dell was crying. "I never ever wanted to. Little Arthur made us."

"Good heavens," her mother said.

"I think I'm starting to understand," Robert's father said. He seemed old and worried. He looked at Robert. Robert was still staring at the ceiling. "It was all Eugene's idea," he said. "Eugene made him up."

Eugene sat in a big blue chair. He looked small and white, and he sounded scared. "I didn't make him up, either," he said in a long slow voice. "He just came. He came and sat on my bed and told me stuff. And he isn't bad. He's nice," Eugene said, going slower and slower. "He's so nice. He thought up all these great things to do. The next thing would have been the best one yet. We were going to initiate these new kids. He said to make them lie down in the new highway and count to fifty out loud before they moved. Out loud. That would have been a good test, all right, to see how brave they were. That would have been so nice, it would have been so much fun. Little Arthur always has these good ideas, see. He's real smart. He thinks of everything. It sure would have been fun. He's so nice. They would have laid down in the highway."

Robert's father was looking at Robert's mother and Sara Dell's mother, and when they made little noises he said for Eugene to come on, that he would take him back to his aunt's house in a car; but Eugene jerked away from Robert's father and ran across the room with us all there and watching. "He's really nice," Eugene said.

"Well," Robert's father said like he was in a business meeting, "tomorrow you are to go up to Mrs. Tate's and apologize to her and help her fix her rose bed. Is that understood? She'll be expecting you. O.K.?" We nodded our heads.

"There's one more thing," Robert's father said. "Little Arthur is dead. Do you understand that? He's dead. There is no more Little Arthur."

"There is so!" yelled Baby Julia.

"There is NOT," Robert's father said. His face was hard. "Little Arthur died. He's dead."

"How come?" asked Baby Julia.

"Because I killed him," Robert's father said, and we all drew back from him. But I knew he was lying. I wished I didn't know it, but I did.

Then, "That's a lie," Eugene said, loud. He looked up at Robert's father. "Nobody can kill him but me. And I won't, so there."

"He's dead," Robert's father said it like a fact, like two and two is four.

"You're crazy," said Eugene. "Sir," he added.

We were all quiet except for Sara Dell, who was still crying out loud. "Come on, Julia," said Robert's father. "I'll take you home when I take Eugene to his aunt's house."

"Her mother must be frantic," said Sara Dell's mother. "She's only six."

"No, I called," Robert's mother told her.

"Please can I have another Hershey bar," said Baby Julia, but she didn't get one. She walked along behind Eugene who was walking along behind Robert's father. Eugene looked like he was walking in his sleep and he didn't look back. Baby Julia did, though. She waved.

"Go to bed," Robert's father said from the door, and Robert went upstairs running all the way.

"Good night," Sara Dell's mother said to Robert's.

"Wait a minute," I said. "Wait a minute. Aren't you going to do anything to me? I took off my pants and played Iron Lung. I did. And Little Arthur and Eugene were on top of me and they were the Iron Lung. They went up and down and I was dying. I was dying. Aren't you going to do anything to me? I didn't have any shorts or even any pants on. What about that? I hurt. I hurt down there. What about that?" I kept talking faster and faster and I couldn't quit.

"It's all right, Susan," Sara Dell's mother said. She patted me.

"It's not all right," I said. "What're you going to do? Aren't you going to spank me or anything?"

"Hush, Susan," they said. "It's all right."

"Of course we won't spank you," said Robert's mother.

"Why not?" I asked. "Why won't you spank me?" I couldn't shut up.

"Good night," said Robert's mother. She kissed me. I didn't want her to, I wanted to get whipped with a whip but nobody would do it and I went home with Sara Dell. There were a lot of things I had to think about but I didn't have time to do it because the bed smelled good and I was so tired I hurt all over, so I went right to sleep. I didn't even try to say my prayers.

I had a funny dream and when I told Sara Dell about it in the morning she laughed. I dreamed that the fingernail on my right thumb started growing and growing and I couldn't make it stop growing. Betty filed it with a file but the fingernail was so hard that the file split right in two. Then Sara Dell came in with some scissors, but they didn't work either. Frank tried to cut it with great big clippers like he uses on the bushes in the palace garden. The clippers were so big they scared me, and they broke right in two. Frank took them away. The Queen was there but she was sitting in a high tree, a funny tree with pink leaves like feathers, and she was laughing. She never came down. Little Arthur came, and pointed at me, and then he went away also, and men came with signs that said, DO NOT TOUCH THIS GIRL. HER FINGERNAIL IS TOO LONG. They put the signs in the ground all around me and hung a rope around the signs so that no one could come near me. I sat in the rope cage and sometimes people brought me candy and peanuts while I got very, very old and my thumbnail grew so long that it went almost all the way around the whole earth. It was still growing when I woke up.

For the week after that I stayed mostly with Sara Dell and sometimes at home, and Betty and Daddy were always away. Elsie Mae was there but she was quieter and I thought she was growing smaller all the time. I went into the kitchen one day when Elsie Mae was making bread. She put all the flour in a round silver pot and shook the pot, and the flour came out soft as air through the little holes in the bottom of the pot. It looked real pretty coming down and piling up in white piles on the waxed paper. It looked so pretty I cried.

"That's the way people are," Elsie Mae said. "You can shake 'em up and move them around any which way you feel like, but it all comes out the same way in the end. Don't do no good at all." Elsie Mae shook her head and made little clicking noises with her mouth. I went away from the kitchen then because I couldn't stand to look at Elsie Mae's shoes. They were the bright silver ones, like the Queen used to have and maybe still had, someplace away from here.

A lot of things reminded me of the Queen but I had a new trick of how not to think about those things. I had fixed my mind up so it was cut into boxes, sort of like the boxes eggs come in. In one box I put the Queen; and in one box I put Little Arthur, who was not dead either but alive all the time and I knew it; and in the other boxes I put the things I liked, like God and Sara Dell and Baby Julia and the dogbushes and the way the wading house was before the flood. That way, if I ever wanted to think about anything I could just pull it out of its box and roll it around in the part of my head that was not boxed in. When I got tired of it I could close it back up in its box, and there were some things that I never took out of their boxes at all. I took the dogbushes out then, and thought about them, and I liked them so much that I went out there to sit.

It was quiet except for the bees talking in the dogbush flowers. Frank was working in the castle garden, cutting extra leaves off rosebushes. Sara Dell walked around in her yard with yellow hair in the sun, and I almost yelled at her to come over but I didn't. We didn't talk much any more because there were too many things not to talk about. The club was gone even though Little Arthur was still around, and there was nobody much to play with. Baby Julia was at the beach and

and Robert was at baseball practice all the time now since it had started, and Gregory had a new dog, and Eugene had gone back to the city real fast without telling anybody goodbye.

I sat all by myself under the dogbushes and played with my mind. I took Sara Dell's mother and my daddy out of their boxes to try to figure out that thing they had said to each other. I had heard them the night before. Sara Dell's mother said, "I'm really concerned about Susan, Max. She stares at things so much now. And I've never seen her cry about her mother's leaving. Has she ever cried?"

"No," Daddy had said, "not that I know of. I'm a little worried about her myself."

"I think she should cry," Sara Dell's mother had said. "It's not natural."

I didn't know what wasn't natural and I didn't know why I should cry. Babies cry. Besides, the Queen was better off, and I was glad we had had her for as long as we did. Sure I missed her, but by then I didn't know exactly that I was missing the Queen and knew only that I was missing. Sometimes I would get very busy with how much I was missing, and that's when I would stare.

I put Sara Dell's mother and my daddy back into their boxes, and then I thought I would look at the prettiest box I had. All of Daddy's pictures were in this box. I took them out and looked at them one by one. I couldn't go down to the basement to see them any more because Daddy had moved them all away. He had a new job at the college, and he had taken them all over there except for one. That was the little girl who looked like me, and she was in the living room. After I looked at all the pictures in my head I put them back into their box and went inside to see the little girl in the living room.

I stood and looked at her for a while, and then I heard somebody calling my name. "What?" I yelled. "Yes?" But nobody was there. Elsie Mae was gone from the kitchen and nobody was there. I thought it had probably been God or Little Arthur and I didn't much care which. I stood in the living room and waited for them to call again, but nobody called me. I waited a long time, right in the middle of the living room because I knew that there was something else left to happen, and I didn't know what it was, but that was not the day.

Summer went on into the days when the sun goes down sooner and you have to wear socks to play outside at night. Betty was going back to college, and getting engaged, and she kept Elsie Mae busy getting all her clothes ready for everything. Betty was very nice to me. I sat around mostly, or went swimming at the big pool with Sara Dell and the new kids.

One day I was coming home from swimming, all wrapped up in a pink towel because it was five o'clock in the afternoon and sort of cold, and I stopped in front of the castle for not any reason at all and looked at the castle for a long time because there was something wrong with it. "Come on in," yelled Elsie Mae from the front door. "You'll catch your death standing out there wet like that."

When I was dry and tingly, I thought what it was that was different. It was Frank. Frank had been in the yard so much that he was a part of the yard, but this afternoon he wasn't there. That's why the yard looked so funny.

"Where's Frank?" I said to Elsie Mae who was putting on a coat to go over to Ella Mae's because it was her night off from work.

"Frank?" said Elsie Mae. "Frank? What you know about Frank?"

"I don't know anything," I said. I ate an animal cracker that was a bear with one foot gone. "What about him?"

"He died," said Elsie Mae.

"He did what?" I said. I almost choked on my animal cracker.

"He died," said Elsie Mae.

"Died." I said after her. "Died?"

"Dead as a doornail," Elsie Mae said. "What's the matter with you, child?" I didn't say anything. I couldn't believe that Frank had died. I was really mad at him for it. I ate another animal cracker and this time it was a dog, and I asked Elsie Mae how he did it, how he died.

"He just up and died," Elsie Mae said. "That's all."

Then she went to see her sister and I went out to sit under the dogbushes.

It was getting dark but the sun went away so slowly that things were not really dark or light either one, and everything was green. Some things were darker green than others, and when I looked at my legs out in front of me on the ground they were light, light green. All the dogbushes were full of their flowers but the bees were already in bed.

I couldn't believe that Frank was dead. Frank couldn't die, because he was like the roses and the trees and the grass and everything else in the castle garden. That's all he was, and Frank couldn't die any more than a tree could die. He didn't have the right to die but he had done it, he had died anyway. Frank had fooled the

Queen; and Frank had fooled God and laughed, pushing that lawn mower around and around the tree; and Frank had even fooled the government; and then Frank had just gone away and died. It was awful.

Daddy came to the back door and yelled for me to come in and dress to go out to dinner. "In a minute," I said. "Just a minute," and Daddy went back into the house.

I sat under the dogbushes and it was green, green all over the world. Everything was blooming hard and fast because it knew that soon it would have to die. Fireflies came out but there were not many of them, not as many as there had been at the first of the summer, and every firefly was like a little part of the Queen. The morning that summer started I ate Post Toasties. The Queen was there and the Princess who wasn't a Princess any more, but only Betty and engaged, and it was the first morning of summer that Eugene came. It was all long ago and past and I could only remember the little things. Like Eugene's eyes, I could remember them. And the pictures, and the way Baby Julia ate grass, and roses, but the roses were all dead now or dying, and Frank was already dead. The wind blew and made me cold, and I thought about the dogs.

"Come on in, Susan," yelled Daddy from the door.

Frank was like a rock, a tree or a rock, and he was dead. Then while I sat there, that hard green light of dying blew up in me like a flashbulb and I started shaking in my stomach because everything was dying and because then I knew that I was too. I will die; you will die; he, she, it will die. I tried to pray to God but I couldn't pray because I couldn't remember any prayers at all. I watched one firefly but it never moved and when I knew it was a star I prayed to it. "Dear star in heaven," I prayed. "Dear star, star, star." That was all I said but I said it over and over through the clear green air straight up to heaven. The star started to move, it danced in the sky, it winked at me and nodded, and the hard things in my stomach went away.

Next I did a funny thing. I looked down from the star to the tops of the trees and I said "Dear tops of the trees, dear trees, trees, trees," over and over again until I was praying to the trees and they were talking to me. I laughed and laughed. I sat under the dogbushes with everything green and dying around me in the end of summer and I prayed to the grass and to the flowers and to the rocks and to everything, and everything talked back to me and it was all the same. It didn't matter what I prayed to.

"Oh, great picnic table," I said. "Oh, white picnic table, please bless me," and the picnic table blessed me. It was all the same.

"Come on, Susan," Daddy called for the last time from the back door. "Let's go."

I went on my hands and knees out of the dogbushes and stood up. Everything talked to me, it was all the same, they wrapped me up in their green talking like a Christmas present. I could pray to anything. When I got to the steps I turned around and looked one time back into the outside. Little Arthur was under the dogbushes now and I was not surprised. I understood then that wherever I went, for maybe the whole rest of my life, Little Arthur would not be very far away. He would be somewhere close outside. I knew that he would always be there, but it didn't scare me.

Daddy was sitting inside very quiet, smoking a cigarette and waiting for me and I loved him then so much that I almost fell down on the steps. The green things from outside pushed in on my skin, and Little Arthur came out from the bushes and stood on the grass, looking at me. "Oh, wooden steps," I prayed, but nothing mattered. The steps were solid under me and it was all right. Mother had left us and Betty was engaged and Frank had died. Daddy sat in a little lake of light from a living-room lamp, and all of a sudden I was very hungry. I turned around and smiled at Little Arthur to show him that I wasn't afraid any more. Then I went upstairs and put on my new yellow dress and my new red shoes without straps and I went out to dinner with Daddy.

$\mathcal{V}$OICES OF THE $\mathcal{S}$OUTH